Blue Ridge Mountain Escape

Rebecca Bridges

Printed and Bound in the United States of America

Cover and Interior design: Rebecca Bridges/Outboard Publishing LLC

First printing September 2016

ISBN: 978-0-9975718-2-0

DEDICATION

I dedicate this novella to my children and their families. The inspiration for this book came from the Christmas we spent in a cabin in the Blue Ridge Mountains. Thank goodness we didn't run into any bank robbers!

CONTENTS

Acknowledgements

Chapter One	1
Chapter Two	9
Chapter Three	20
Chapter Four	29
Chapter Five	41
Chapter Six	50
Chapter Seven	60
Chapter Eight	64
Chapter Nine	66
Chapter Ten	69
Chapter Eleven	76
Chapter Twelve	83
Chapter Thirteen	86
Chapter Fourteen	93
Chapter Fifteen	97
Chapter Sixteen	99
Chapter Seventeen	101
Chapter Eighteen	104
Chapter Nineteen	107
Chapter Twenty	110
About the Author	113

Mary

Enjoy your trip to the mountains!

Ruben

Bridge

ACKNOWLEDGMENTS

As always, many thanks to my husband for his reminders to *take a break* as well as his support in pursuit of my writing dream.

A heartfelt thank you to all the members of the Coastal Authors Network and Carolina Forest Authors Club. Your support, enthusiasm and critiques helped me complete this manuscript.

Betty Bolte, my editor and friend, your help made this novella the best it could be. Thank you for all the pointers and keeping the faith.

CHAPTER ONE

After a week of solitude Trevor Montgomery felt refreshed and almost human. He stood in the tiny kitchen of the Blue Ridge Mountain cabin he'd rented for two weeks and flipped the trout he fried as he heard a noise. It took a moment to recognize the banging as a knock at the door. Turning off the fire under his fish, he strode to the entrance. Frowning, he glanced out the window and didn't see a car. How had the person gotten here?

Jerking open the door, he simultaneously asked, "What?" He felt more than annoyed to have his self-imposed seclusion interrupted.

Before him stood a tall, slender woman. Her nose was a little too short, a few freckles sprinkled across it, and her hairline was too far back, making her forehead seem too large. Not beautiful in the traditional sense, but attractive. She had curly red hair pulled back in a ponytail and huge green eyes blinking at his sudden appearance. She wore a pair of jeans so tight they could have been sprayed on to legs that went on forever. He pictured big breasts beneath her bulky jacket. His member thickened as he watched her lick her lips and her eyes dart to the left.

She waved her left hand wrapped in a dish towel. “Help. I need help.” The makeshift bandage had red splotches of blood on it. “I need a doctor. Could you drive me to town?” She constantly glanced to her left. When he glanced in that direction, he saw nothing. Maybe she had some kind of eye problem.

Suspicious, but unable to determine her true motive, he said, “Come in. I can take care of it for you. I’ve done first aid plenty of times.”

“No!” Her response came out as a shout. “Sorry, no.” Her voice quieted. “I mean I need stitches and I lost a lot of blood. I may need a transfusion or something.” He noticed she kept looking toward her left and frowning. Her demeanor became panicky. She turned her face to the left, her eyes grew even larger, her mouth opened, but no sound erupted.

He grabbed the front of her jacket, jerked her inside, and slammed the door a split second before bullets thumped into the space where they’d been standing.

Trevor slipped the bar across the door then sped to the back door to secure it.

“Close the shutters,” he yelled while closing the one in the kitchen. He raced to the bedroom and closed the wooden slats in that room. The unmistakable sound of breaking glass came from the bathroom. He snatched his 9mm from the nightstand, dropped to the floor, and then belly crawled to the bathroom door. Keeping his body out of the doorway, he stretched his arm to shoot his weapon toward the window. A screech followed by a thump sounded as something landed outside.

"You asshole. You'll pay for this," a man shouted. Shots came through the window accompanied by more cussing and yelling.

After a few moments of silence Trevor crawled the rest of the way into the bathroom. He avoided the glass littering the floor as he closed the shutter. Racing back into the living room he found the woman had done as instructed, then she'd shoved the couch to block the door and sat on the floor leaning against it. Thank God, she wasn't crying. He could handle most anything, but not female tears.

"How many are there?" He joined her on the floor. He kept his voice low so the men outside wouldn't hear them.

"Two," she said, with a staccato-like response as she glanced at him.

"How many weapons?"

She continued her business-like retort. "At least a couple of pistols, they're 9mm semi-automatics, an Uzi, and a couple of knives. That's what I saw. There could be more."

"The Uzi could be trouble. Do you know what they want?" Their lives depended on whether they could diffuse the situation.

"A car. They drove theirs off the road sometime before dawn and don't have a way out. They assumed my cabin wasn't occupied since they didn't see a vehicle or boat. They broke in and helped themselves to my food during my morning stroll. All of us were surprised when I opened the back door and there they were."

Trevor awkwardly patted her shoulder. "The good

news is they didn't kill you."

She snorted. "Not yet. They were pretty pissed when I told them I didn't know where they could find a car. Once they searched my place, they argued for more than an hour about what to do. They devised this plan to have me be a female in distress. Figured I'd get more sympathy than them."

Trevor chuckled. "That's true. Thanks for trying to warn me."

"I didn't know what else to do." She sounded like she was about to break down. "I knew one of them watched me so I couldn't be too obvious."

Again he patted her shoulder. "You did great."

"Only because you reacted so fast." She gave him a tremulous smile. "Otherwise, we'd both be dead."

He wanted to distract her for a moment to calm her nerves. "So, what's your name?"

"Madison, Madison Hendricks."

"I'm Trevor Montgomery. Which cabin are you renting?"

"It's about two miles north of here."

"Why don't you have a vehicle?" He questioned her unusual situation. They were in the middle of nowhere for cryin' out loud.

"No, my dad dropped me off. He won't be back to pick me up for a few days."

"Since there's no cell service up here we need to consider the options."

She needed a distraction to keep her from dwelling on their unpleasant reality. "With all the shutters closed it's dark in here. I'll grab some candles." He crawled over to the fireplace then stood up for the seconds it took to snatch candles from the mantle.

"Since all the windows are shut and covered, do we need to stay on the floor?" Madison asked.

"Yeah. This way, if they start shooting at the windows, we'll have furniture for cover. Not knowing what kind of ammo they have, it'll be safer here." Trevor dug a lighter out of his pocket and lit the two candles. "There, that's better. I have more candles in the bedroom." He made it a statement to see if Madison needed the security of additional light.

"No need right now. Better save the others in case we're here for a long time."

He liked the way she thought about conserving their meager resources.

She scrunched her face. "By the way, how come this house has shutters on the inside? It's something I haven't seen before."

The talk about something other than the two men outside appeared to calm her.

"Bears. The owners had some black bears break in one fall. When they arrived for a Thanksgiving week celebration the mess upset the lady of the house."

She tilted her head and frowned. "That doesn't explain why they didn't put the shutters on the outside."

Trevor gave a chuckle. "She said it would ruin the outside appearance. Also, she figured if more bears arrived during their time here, it would be easier and safer if the shutters were inside."

For the first time he saw Madison smile. It almost blinded him.

"I suppose it makes some kind of sense." She shook her head. "Although if the aesthetic concerned her I'm surprised she thought the shutters looked better inside than out."

"I wondered about that, too. Notice all the shutters are covered by curtains. No doubt her husband wanted to make her feel safe, so didn't argue. Now I'm happy she had the crazy idea."

"Absolutely."

Trevor's thoughts veered away from the current situation to the closeness of the woman next to him. It had been way too long since he'd had female companionship. He'd need to keep his mind off her or he'd embarrass himself with the natural reaction.

Now that he'd calmed her nerves, he needed to find out more about their opponents. "I'm assuming these guys are on the run from something. Any ideas what?"

"I haven't been listening to the news. No television or radio. However, I remember the day we drove up here a local station reported a bank robbery in Atlanta. They shot someone when fleeing the scene. Maybe it's them and they're hiding out here."

"It's as good an explanation as any. Whatever their situation, they won't want us as witnesses. If they shot someone, they'd be desperate. Desperate men make bad decisions."

"So what should we do? Give them your keys and let them drive away? What will we do? Hoof it to town?"

Her obvious dismay made Trevor want to fix their problem. Now. "I could toss them my keys. If they leave, then we'll need to walk down to town." He'd had a switch installed to keep thieves from taking his vehicle. It cut the engine after a mile if you didn't turn it off before starting the car. The fact he hadn't turned it on had been a major oversight. He'd never make the same mistake again.

"Are there any other cabins nearby?" Before he could answer, she asked, "How come we haven't heard them shooting or yelling at us?"

Hearing the rise of panic in her voice, he answered only the first question. "The nearest cabin other than the one you are staying in is about four miles the other direction and you have to know where you're going. There's barely a trail. No one there right now. Town is about fifty miles away; you drove through it on the way here."

"We did go through a small town, but I didn't pay attention as to the distance."

The distraction worked and she sounded less panicky.

"A long hike." He hesitated a moment. "In answer to your other question, why haven't we heard them? I'm guessing the shots I fired hit one of them and they're tending to the injuries. We'll hear soon enough." Trying to alleviate any further questions, he said, "Before we do, let's talk about a plan."

He shifted on the hard floor to gaze directly at her. "The best way to make them leave is to give them my keys. However, I don't like the idea of letting them loose on other people in the area. I'm sure they plan to pick an unoccupied cabin and settle in. If they meet with resistance I have no doubt they'll kill." He frowned at the admission. "I don't want that on my conscious."

Those eyes of hers again grew large at his comment.

"Once they leave what can we do? There is no cell service or wi-fi in the area."

He pursed his lips. "You mentioned you planned to stay another week before someone picked you up. I can't believe you intended to stay up here the whole time without some way to contact people if a problem arose."

Her expression became troubled. "You're right. I had a satellite phone."

Trevor perked up with hope. "Is it still at your place?"

"No." She huffed with annoyance. "They found it when I returned from my morning stroll. They kept it, but took the battery out. They didn't want anyone tracking it."

"Then they're smarter than I'd given them credit." He let out a sigh with his comment. A new idea came to mind. "If we give them my keys then follow them, I can contact authorities once I catch up to them."

"Follow them? Catch up to them on foot?" Her voice raised a notch with her reply. "Are you out of your mind? If it were even possible they'd kill us."

Trevor corrected her. "Not us. Me. You have two choices, stay here or make it to town on your own."

CHAPTER TWO

Madison couldn't believe his plan. "So on foot you plan to track down two men in a car with an arsenal of weapons. Alone. Then tie them up and haul them to the nearest sheriff. All the while I'll hoof it down a mountain road. Alone. While bears and who knows what other wild animals are nearby. When I make it to town I tell them you're up here someplace being a hero. So we all stand around and wait for you to drive into town with the two would-be killers?"

"If you know how to shoot, I can give you one of my guns." Trevor's grin caused her stomach to flutter. "When you say it like that I suppose it does sound a bit crazy."

"Crazy? Ya think? How do you propose to track someone in a car?" Madison tried to concentrate on their conversation. It took a major effort with the buff mountain man sitting so close to her. His short beard and even shorter hair told her he would normally have a clean shaven face and head. When he answered the door, she'd judged his height to be at least two inches over six feet. She had to look up at him, which didn't happen often with her five-foot-ten frame. His quick reaction saved both their lives. Her first response when he'd grabbed her jacket had been to wrap her arms and legs around him. Good thing there hadn't been time. Thinking about it made her temperature rise.

"That's easy. They have two directions to go."

It took Madison a moment due to her daydreaming to match his answer with the question she'd asked.

"If they drive back toward your cabin they won't go more than another four miles before it dead ends, then have to turn back this way. We know they won't want to travel all the way back to town and take the chance of the cops seeing them. I'm sure they're trying to figure out how to escape Georgia without going through a town. They must not have planned anything after leaving Atlanta. There are four other turnoffs between here and town. I'll check each turnoff to see which one they picked. Since they ran into a ditch last night, they probably won't want to drive after dark. I should be able to track them down in a few hours."

It took her a minute to make a decision. "When you explain it, then it doesn't sound as crazy," she replied using his own words back at him. "There's one change you need to make."

He tilted his head and frowned. "What?"

"I'm not walking fifty miles to town. I'm going with you. And, yes, I know how to use a gun." She could handle herself. She'd done fine so far, under the circumstances.

"Just because you know how to use a gun doesn't mean you can come with me." Trevor's commanding tone made her grind her teeth.

She blew out a deep breath. "And why not?"

At that moment they heard one of the men shout, "Give us your keys and we'll leave you alone."

Trevor shouted back in a whiny voice she hadn't heard him use before. "How do I know you won't shoot us once you have the keys?"

He dropped his voice to a whisper. "I want them to think we're scared."

The reply came quickly. "No reason for us to. Throw out the keys and we'll be out of here before you know it."

"You can't leave us here without a car. How will we get help?"

How had he made his voice sound weak and scared?

They heard the two men arguing before one responded. "We'll call 911 for you when we have cell service."

"How stupid do they think we are?" Madison asked in a hushed voice.

"All right. All right." Trevor's voice sounded resigned when he yelled a response. "Be sure to let them know I've got a bullet wound and need an ambulance." He lowered his voice for Madison, "They won't think we're a threat."

She shoved the couch away from the door being sure to make a lot of noise so the men outside would hear. While she moved furniture, Trevor checked the slit in the two windows to make sure the men hadn't come close to the house. He pulled the keys out of his pocket, unbarred the door, motioned Madison to open the door a couple of inches, and then he tossed the keys without making himself a target. Madison immediately slammed the door shut and put the bar back down. His SUV sat close to the front door, but the keys landed short. Trevor and Madison watched as the men took a long tree limb to pull the keys toward them. The men were smart enough to realize they'd be unprotected if they strode out into the yard to pick them up.

As the men climbed into the SUV, Madison noticed one of them had a makeshift bandage around one arm. So one of them had been hit by a bullet, or cut by the glass from the bathroom window.

"They're heading up toward your cabin. We need to gather our stuff. They'll be back in ten to fifteen minutes. I want to be ready to follow when they head back down." Trevor raced to the bedroom.

"You're serious about tracking them?" Madison followed in his wake.

"Of course." Trevor rummaged through items in the bedroom. "Are you serious about going with me?"

"Yes. I won't stand by and let those men hurt anyone else. Staying here would drive me insane in the circumstances and trudging fifty miles not knowing who or what I'd run into sounds foolish. I won't hold you back. You can always use me to create a diversion or something."

He stood still, staring at her the same way her father used to do. "You'll have to do exactly what I say when I say it. Agreed?"

It took a lot of willpower not to make a snarky comeback. "Yes."

"I don't like it, but I see your point about staying here or going to town." He tossed a flannel shirt at her. "You'll need this, and the temperature will drop once the sun sets." He picked up a small backpack and tossed it to her as well. "Fill that up with some food and water. I'll put the other gear together."

Madison didn't like being ordered around, but it would be in her best interest to do as he said. For now. She took off her jacket and put both the shirt and jacket on a hook next to the door. When they left, she'd put the jacket on and tied the shirt around her waist. Later, when it got cold, she'd put it on under her jacket. In the kitchen she found jerky, a couple of oranges, bread, cheese, trail mix, and a couple of large bottles of water. Noticing the half-cooked fish on the stove, she knew it would draw bugs and maybe some animals. She opened the back door, tossed it outside, and then secured the exit. He'd also sliced some tomatoes, so she made a couple of tomato sandwiches they could eat now before starting their trek.

Trevor marched into the living room and dumped some gear on the floor next to the door. "You said you know how to use a gun. What kind?" He put a Glock 9mm in his jacket pocket and hung it on a peg next to hers.

"I've experience with semi-automatics like the Glock you put in your pocket as well as a Sig Sauer and Ruger. If you have a rifle, I can manage a Weatherby Vanguard or Winchester Model 70 if it has the M.O.A. Trigger System." Madison had the satisfaction of seeing his eyebrows go up with her response.

"Guess you do know something about guns." Trevor lowered his voice and narrowed his eyes. "So have you shot anything other than targets?"

She understood his real question. "Yes, I've hunted with my father, uncles, and cousins, going after deer, rabbits, and squirrels. If you're really asking will I shoot a human? If it means me or them, I plan to be the one left standing."

"Then you're welcome to one of my Glocks and the Weatherby." He pulled out each weapon from one of the bags on the floor. "I'll hang on to the Remington R-15."

"Right. I also know a few bird calls. An owl and bobwhite, if we need to signal each other."

"I'll keep that in mind."

She accepted the weapons, setting the Glock on the counter next to the backpack after checking the safety and slinging the rifle over her shoulder. "Do you always carry this much fire power?"

Shrugging, he didn't glance her way when he responded. "I've been doing a little target practice while I've been up here."

"So those shots fired earlier wouldn't bring anyone here to investigate?"

"No." He handed her a couple of small boxes. "Here's some ammo for those."

Madison took the boxes and added them to the food in the backpack. She handed him a sandwich. "Let's eat while we wait."

"Good idea. I'm starving." He grabbed the proffered food. "I didn't eat lunch."

"I noticed. Neither did I." She strode the few steps to the couch, swung the rifle off her shoulder, propped it next to her, sat down, and took a bite of the sandwich.

Before she had time to take a second bite, Trevor finished, stood up, and went to the window. "Thanks, that was great." He gazed out toward the road. "They should be driving back down soon. When you finish you might want to take a trip to the bathroom. This could be your last chance at indoor plumbing for a day or two."

She'd been thinking the same thing. Wasting no time, she made the trip and snagged a roll of toilet paper to add to the backpack. She opened the door of a small closet in the bathroom and snagged a broom and dust pan. Sweeping up the glass from beneath the window gave her some time to think about everything that had happened the last few hours.

It could have turned out a lot worse if Trevor hadn't reacted so fast. His reflexes, physique, abilities with a gun, the way he planned to track the two men, all reminded her of her father, a retired army lieutenant colonel. The orders and expectation of perfection had grated on her nerves as a teenager. Now she appreciated the discipline and preparation. Madison took a moment to brush her hair and put it back into a ponytail, and then wash her face and hands.

As she hurried back into the living room, he asked, "Do you have a hat and gloves with you?"

She rearranged things in the backpack. "Yes, in my jacket." She put the Glock in the right pocket of her jacket.

He returned to watching out the window.

"So what army outfit are you with?"

"Huh?" He mumbled without taking his eyes off his target.

"What unit?"

"How did you figure it out?" She could hear the grin in his voice.

"It wasn't difficult. My dad is retired. You remind me of him. At least the way you give orders." She couldn't keep the snarky comment from coming out of her mouth.

"I'm stationed at Ft. Benning." He kept watch out the window.

"So you're armor, infantry, or ranger, right?" She knew it. Her father had been stationed there a few years ago.

"Yeah."

"So which unit? Infantry?" For some reason, she didn't think he was armor like her father.

"You're pretty good at guessing. Which one do you think?"

"Ranger. Am I right?" She heard a vehicle outside.

Trevor stood straight and silent. "There they go. Let's load up and head out."

Taking only moments to put on their jackets, Madison slipped on the backpack and slung the rifle over her shoulder. Trevor had combined the sleeping bag and a satchel, which she assumed held more guns, ammo, and other gear, like a backpack and shrugged into it. He took the bar off the front door and grabbed the other rifle as he stepped outside.

"We'll use the road until we arrive at the first turn off." Trevor set a fast pace. "Then we'll need to stay out of sight."

"We could miss an opportunity to catch a ride with someone."

"Unlikely. Not many people live this far up the mountain. The closer to dusk most people stay inside. As our two friends found out last night, it's easy to run off the road."

"You never did say if you were a ranger or infantry." She still wanted to know. His long legs and pace made her switch to a slow jog to keep up.

"No, I didn't," he continued without breathing hard. "Once we leave the main road we'll need to keep our voices low. We don't want to announce our presence to those guys or the wild animals."

"I don't suppose you have some night vision goggles in your bag? Otherwise, we could step off a cliff or something." She'd said it sarcastically, not expecting him to have any.

"Yep, I do. You'll need to hold on to my backpack when dark comes. Wouldn't want to lose you."

In no time at all they arrived at the first turnoff. When Trevor knelt down to inspect the tire tracks she gladly stopped. They'd been traveling at a fast clip and she appreciated the break. The paved road they were on veered off to a dirt-and-gravel trail. Even to her, it was obvious a car had turned this way recently. The question in her mind, was it the right car?

"See the tread on the left?"

"Yes. What about it?" It didn't appear any different than any other tire tread she'd seen.

"I had a nail in my left rear, tire so I had it removed and patched." He pointed to a void in the tread pattern. "That spot is the patch." Trevor stood up. "We've got 'em now." He grinned at her.

Her hormones hummed at the expression on his face. The tracking and anticipation of what would happen next energized him. And she responded like some groupie seeing her rock star idol.

"I'm not sure we've *got 'em* yet, but at least we know where they're headed." Madison took off her backpack and pulled out the bottle of water. After taking a small swig, she offered it to Trevor.

He took a sip and handed it back. "They can't drive very fast on this road and they sure as hell won't travel on it after dark. The first thing you run into is a rustic camping area. They'll pass it by looking for a cabin."

"You know this area well. Have you checked out all the side roads?"

Nodding, he started walking into the woods and paralleling the road before he answered. "I've considered building a cabin up here."

"Did you buy the one where you're staying?"

"No, renting this time. Family friends own it. I wanted to try the area out before committing. We need to keep quiet. I don't want to take a chance those dirt bags hear us before we see them."

"Right." Madison understood the importance of silence, but it made her more nervous. She liked to talk to keep her mind off unpleasant things. Or write. Writing kept her mind occupied, too. It's why she became an author. She'd think about her current work in progress. Great idea, only her thoughts kept returning to the hunk in front of her. The view from this angle had her wanting to see more. He had one fine backside. She stumbled. He turned and grabbed her arm before she did a face plant.

"Are you all right?" he whispered. His concern appeared genuine. "Is the pace too fast for you?"

"I'm fine." Her reply matched his low voice. Heat flooded her cheeks. She'd been too preoccupied thinking about his ass to watch her step. "Caught my foot on a root. The pace is fine."

"This is a good place to take a break anyway. Let's have a little more water." He traveled a short distance to a clearing and sat on picnic table she hadn't noticed.

Madison joined him and pulled out the bottle and some trail mix from her bag. "A handful of this sounds like a good idea. So is this the camp site you mentioned?" She noticed the area had been cleared of underbrush. She spotted some fire pits and an outhouse.

"Yep, this is it." He took a long swallow of water.

She watched as his Adam's apple bobbed up and down. Now why the hell did that seem sexy? Shaking her head she swapped the bag of trail mix for the bottle of water with him. Munching, she felt the heat from his body. He smelled of smoke and earth. She reminded herself of the promise she'd made in high school that she would have nothing to do with military men.

"Let's get back to it." He put the bag of trail mix back in the pack as she slipped the bottle in.

"Think I'll put the shirt on under my jacket before we start up again. It's starting to cool down." Setting the backpack down, she adjusted her clothing.

CHAPTER THREE

Nodding his reply, Trevor slipped on his gloves and hat. Sitting this close to Madison and breathing in her scent had him thinking of doing things to her, causing his member to spring to attention. Glancing in her direction, he had to close his eyes. She'd taken off her jacket and put on his shirt. The movement made her stretch the material of her sweater across a magnificent chest. Oh, lord, would he survive?

Turning his back, he waited another minute. "Ready?"

"Yes."

He glanced back. "Stuff your hair under your hat. Your hair will shine like a beacon in the dark." Once the words were out of his mouth, he knew he sounded like the lieutenant he was, issuing orders to his troops.

"Fine. Geesh, why are you so grumpy all of a sudden?" She did as he told her.

Little did she know he hadn't been with a woman in more than six months. Frustration could make a man grumpy. When they got out of this mess, he'd take care of that problem.

Dark came early in the mountains. Being the first part of October the temperature wasn't too cold during the day, but it would be close to freezing when night fell. Less than an hour after their break he stopped and whispered, "You'll need to grab hold of my backpack when we start up again." He took off his pack and pulled out the night vision goggles. "I'll slow down. The animals will start coming out. I don't want to tangle with anything if we can avoid them."

Madison took off her pack and pulled out the bottle of water. Taking a drink she passed it to him without a word. When he finished he handed it back and they both put their packs back on.

He leaned over and patted her arm. "We should be getting close to the first cabin. I'm betting these guys stopped here. You're doing great. I'm going to hold my rifle in a ready position." He felt a bit awkward with her after his erotic thoughts. As he put on the goggles and adjusted them, he considered their situation. It wasn't new to him, but he normally had trained men accompanying him. A civilian woman made things more uncertain. When they had started on this journey he'd made up his mind she'd be safer with him than staying alone in the cabin. Not with these two guys on the loose. No telling if they would have doubled back to make sure there were no witnesses or kept going. He'd put her someplace safe before he approached the shooters.

Placing her hand on his backpack he spoke directly in her ear. "If you need to stop, tap my left arm twice. If you see something, tap once and point." When she nodded her understanding they crept forward. Progress slowed and his awareness of her grew. He admired the fact she didn't complain and kept up with him. It took another hour or so before he spotted something other than wild life. Changing directions, he moved toward the structure. Sure enough, there stood his SUV next to a cabin.

Stopping, he removed her hand from his pack. "I see a cabin and my SUV over there." He pointed to their left. "I'm going to take you to a safe place before I approach."

She put her backpack on the ground then took her rifle off her shoulder. "I'm going with you."

"No. You'll stay where I put you."

"I can give you cover."

"I doubt I'll need it. I plan to make my way into the cabin and remove their weapons. They're probably asleep."

"What?" Her eyes grew wide at his pronouncement. "You can't go inside. What if the door squeaks? Or you step on a creaky floor board? They could wake up and shoot you."

"You said you'd do what I told you. And I'm telling you to come with me and stay where I tell you." At her stubborn silence, he relented. "I'll leave my goggles with you so you can watch what's happening. Close your eyes then take them off if a light comes on. You'll be blind for a minute or two."

"All right. If I see you're in trouble, I'll move to your car. At least if they shoot you, I won't let them take off."

He heard the reluctance in her voice. Knowing her scenario would never happen, he agreed. "Stay here a minute until I find a good spot for you." He scanned the area and noticed a downed tree. Before showing her, he checked it out to make sure there weren't any animals using it for a den. When he returned for her she appeared ready and he indicated where she could sit with a view of the front. He took off his pack and set it beside her. "Here, sit on the sleeping bag. The cold ground will make you colder. Don't come running up to the cabin unless I signal for you."

"Yes, sir." She saluted.

He stared at her. "You won't shoot unless I tell you. Right?"

She shook her head. "I won't agree. What I will promise is, I won't shoot anyone unless I'm threatened. I doubt they'll expect me to be out here."

"I don't intend to tell them about you if for some reason they overpower me. So stay out of sight and take off if that happens. Understand?"

"Got it."

He took a mental picture of the path he needed to take to the cabin. No major obstacles appeared to be in the way, so he removed his goggles and handed them to her. He helped her adjust them before leaving. With one handgun in his right pocket, ammo in his left, and his Remington rifle in his hands, he felt confident the two men in the cabin would not be a problem.

Using all the stealth he'd learned in the army, he made his way to the SUV. He reached under the chassis and flipped a switch. Even if they managed to get away from him, they'd only make it a mile.

Continuing to creep toward the cabin, he tried to peer in the windows. As luck would have it, they hadn't bothered to pull the curtains. Why would they? It was dark as pitch outside and they didn't think anyone was about. The glow of embers in the fireplace enabled him to see well enough to make out where the furniture was located in the main room. He also figured out there was only one bedroom. Trying the back door he found it locked. They'd broken in through the front door, but he'd have to cross a porch to reach it. As Madison had pointed out, there could be creaky boards. Stepping slower than ever, he eased onto the porch, then stole toward the door, keeping low in case they woke and jerked off some wild shots.

Keeping his breath slow and steady, he turned the knob on the front door. He eased it open a few inches, then a few more. Barely wide enough to enter, he left it open so as not to take a chance at making more noise. He saw one of the men on the couch and the other on the floor, both had piles of blankets on them. He kept his eyes averted from the glow of the fire. He didn't want to ruin his night vision. Spotting a coffee table pushed out of the way, he noticed they'd put their weapons on it. Grinning at their mistake, he took one at a time and placed them outside on the porch.

Not knowing if they might have other guns inside, he took cover behind an overstuffed chair. "Wake up! Put your hands in the air!"

Startled, the two men sat up and stumbled around trying to reach the weapons that were no longer where they'd left them.

"Hands in the air. I'll shoot!"

Both men turned toward him. One held up both hands and the other stood glaring at him, one arm in a makeshift sling, the other in the air.

Stepping out from behind the chair, he motioned

them to stand in front of the fire. He kicked the blankets out of the way.

The one with the sling asked, "Who the hell are you?"

Trevor kept his weapon pointed at them.

"I'm the guy whose vehicle is outside. The one you stole."

"You?" One of the men said as he furrowed his brow. "We shot you. How'd you get here?"

Ignoring their comments, he opened the door and stepped onto the porch. "Come on in. I've got 'em covered. Be sure to bring all the gear with you." He kept both his eyes and his gun aimed at the two men.

In a moment Madison stepped into the cabin, shut the door, and dropped all the bags at her feet.

"Dig through my pack and find the duct tape. I want you to use it to tie these guys up."

"Hey, you can't do that," the man with the sling insisted. "I've got a bullet in my arm you put there. I need a doctor."

Trevor didn't fall for the line. "If you were so worried, then why didn't you drive to a doctor?"

Giving Trevor a sullen expression, the man with the sling refused to say more.

"You." Trevor motioned with his gun. "The guy with two good hands, move over there and turn your back. Put your arms behind you. You might want to know I have no problems shooting you if you make a wrong move. Got it?" He knew his voice had an edge to it most people would obey.

He was thankful Madison did as told, making sure

she didn't block his line of sight.

"Hey, that's too tight." The man with the sling glared at Madison.

"Wrong. You're trying to keep it loose enough to wiggle out. Not gonna happen."

Trevor noticed Madison tugged the tape even tighter.

When she finished binding the men, Trevor nodded. "Good job, Madison. Thanks. It would have been difficult for me to do it and still keep my gun aimed at them. Okay, boys. What are your names?"

After a pause, one of them said, "We don't have to say nothin' without a lawyer."

"That's right," the other one agreed.

"Well, I'm glad to know you fellas know your rights. Since I'm not a cop it really doesn't matter, but if you don't want me to know your names, no problem. So, Madison, shall we call them Jerk One and Jerk Two?"

Madison grinned. "Let's make Jerk One the fella with only one good hand."

Trevor chuckled then gave his gun to Madison. "Keep this pointed at him. I'm going to take a look at this wound Jerk One has. I want to make sure he's not faking it." Trevor put a couple of logs on the fire and flames shot up giving better light. Then he lighted the oil lamps sitting on the mantle. He found some bottled water in the kitchen and a clean towel.

"Don't touch me." Jerk One started squirming before Trevor put a hand on him.

"Believe it or not I actually know something about gunshot wounds. Let me see how bad it is."

Taking off the man's bandage, he saw how grimy it

was. "We need to clean this out. It'll get infected. You must have put some dirty rag on it."

"I didn't exactly have sterile bandages around." He sneered at Trevor

"I want to make sure you're well enough to stand trial." In spite of the man's protest, Trevor took off the bandage and cleaned the wound. Jerk One shouted his objection the whole time.

"At least it's clean. I'm going out to my car. I have a first aid kit in there with some antiseptic bandages. Madison is going to keep an eye on both of you while I'm gone. She's told me the number of times she's been out with her dad and brothers hunting, and she has a trophy of the time she won the sharp shooter contest in college." He glanced at Madison making an effort to not laugh at his obvious lie. "So don't think about trying to run away. Besides, I'll be right outside with my rifle, and I'm an expert. Understood?"

When both men nodded, he snatched the keys from the coffee table and left the cabin. In no time he'd found the first aid kit and went back inside. Finishing up his task, he noted that Jerk One appeared to have no energy left. Good, he shouldn't cause any trouble. To be safe Trevor went ahead and taped the other leg to the leg of the chair. It would slow him down if he did anything stupid.

"So, Jerk One, where's the satellite phone?" Madison asked.

With no answer she glanced at Trevor. "The place isn't very big. I'll find it."

After a few short minutes Madison returned with it. "Success!" She put the battery into the phone. "I'll call 911.

My dad told me I'd connect with a local dispatcher if I had to call."

"Yes, you will. Tell them we're at the first cabin on Snake Road just off County Road 576."

CHAPTER FOUR

"What's your emergency?" the dispatcher asked.

"We have two men restrained who attacked us earlier today. They may be the bank robbers from Atlanta. Can you send out the sheriff to pick them up?" Madison's admiration for Trevor had gone through the ceiling. When he'd first suggested this plan, she didn't think they'd find the men, much less capture them.

It took several minutes for Madison to convince the dispatcher the call was not a hoax. She also informed them one of the men had been wounded earlier in the day and needed medical attention.

"Yes, fine. It is a satellite phone. You can call back if needed. We'll remain here." She ended the call.

"I'm sure you understood from my side of the conversation the dispatcher was more than skeptical about the call. I'm pretty sure I convinced her that our situation is real. It will be an hour or more before they make it here."

"Not surprising considering the distance." He paused a moment before he continued. "You know when the sheriff arrives they'll have all of us throw out our weapons and walk out with our hands up. Then we'll be searched and handcuffed."

Her eyes grew wide. "No way. We're the ones who called them. That's crazy."

"No, they're being safe. Even though we called they have no idea who did what. Once they sort it all out, we'll be fine." He paused when she stopped shaking her head. "I wanted you to be prepared."

Shock made it take a moment before she could reply. "I'm going to have to wrap my head around it. Good thing you told me. I would have freaked out."

"I'm pretty hungry and you probably are, too. Do you think you could find us something to eat?"

She figured Trevor wanted to keep her busy so as not to think about what would be happening. Under the circumstances she agreed. Madison acted on autopilot. "I know I packed some jerky and bread. Maybe there is something else here in the cabin."

"Hey, man, we'd like something, too," Jerk Two spoke up.

Shc glanced at Trevor and he gave a shake of his head.

Rummaging through the cabinets, she found several plastic containers labeled with various staples, such as flour, sugar, pasta, coffee, and a couple gallons of water and tea. In addition there were some canned goods like tuna, spaghetti sauce, evaporated milk, peanut butter, and even a canned ham. Adding some of the ingredients to what she'd packed they'd have a feast.

First thing she did was make coffee. While it gurgled in the coffee maker, she put a pan of water on to boil, sliced the ham, and opened a can of beans.

As the coffee finished, she asked Trevor, "What do you want in your coffee?"

"I'd ask for some milk, but I'm sure there isn't any," he said offhandedly.

"On the contrary, we have evaporated milk." She opened the can. She'd use the rest for the mac-n-cheese she planned to make.

"Hey, I want a cup. With sugar," Jerk One announced.

"I'll take one with sugar and milk," Jerk Two added.

"Since you have both hands behind your back, I don't know if it'll do you much good," Trevor reminded them.

"Hey, not fair," Jerk one said with a pout.

"What made you think I'm a fair man?" Trevor inquired.

Both men kept whining and complaining.

"If you keep it up I'll put duct tape over your mouths." Trevor glared at the men. They both stared back, but stopped talking.

She felt a bit of guilt as the two men watched them eat. Then she remembered the reason they were in this predicament and shrugged off her concern.

After they finished their meal, Trevor took a final swig of coffee. "Thanks, Madison, I don't think I've eaten better mac-n-cheese."

She could tell he meant it. With the limited supplies she agreed she'd put together a great meal.

All the hiking had made both of them famished. "Glad the cabin owners had a canned ham. I don't think the jerky we brought with us would have been as tasty. We'll have to be sure to replace the food we ate. I'm not certain who owns this cabin, but I sure am glad they keep it stocked." Madison wiped down the counter.

"They must come up here often to keep it supplied like this. I'm glad they didn't happen to be here today."

She turned and cleared the table. "Let me clean up this mess. It shouldn't be too long now before the sheriff or troopers or whatever law enforcement officials are coming to take these guys away."

She stopped her cleaning long enough to throw a couple more logs on to the fire then continued cleanup.

The more Madison thought about her ordeal with these two men, the angrier she became. She glared at the two men. "I don't know what other crimes you'll be charged with, but now they'll add kidnapping. And I'll be happy to testify."

Jerk One scowled directly at Madison and said in a whisper he thought only she could hear. "I'll make sure you regret it. Wait and see. Your time will come."

To his surprise Trevor heard the comment. "Forget about it. If anything happens to her, I'll be coming after you."

Before more words could be exchanged, Madison heard vehicles driving into the area.

The cars came to a halt in such a way as the headlights shown into the cabin. She heard a lot of scrambling about then a spotlight appeared at the back window. "This is the county sheriff. Throw out any weapons you have then come out the front door with your hands on your head."

Trevor opened the cabin door and tossed all the

weapons out except his knife and then cut Jerk One and Jerk Two loose, making them exit the cabin first. Once they were outside, he tossed the knife away from them and closed the door.

He turned to Madison. "It's our turn. Don't worry. Everything will be okay."

She gave him a brave grin. He threw open the door and they both did as instructed.

A medic of some kind worked on Jerk One's injured arm while the other was handcuffed to the gurney he sat on. She heard the man making all kinds of comments claiming he and his friend had been surprised in the cabin by two maniacs. Since Madison knew the scene at the other cabins would prove their side of the story, she didn't even comment.

As Trevor had explained earlier, they were initially treated the same as the two criminals, patting them down, searching for weapons, and then handcuffing them. She and Trevor were separated, which she knew was normal in the situation. Since Trevor had his ID in his wallet, it only took moments for the officers to clear him of any wrong doing. She figured Trevor explained who she was and why she didn't have any ID on her. She provided all her information and, after the two deputies discussed her situation, they released her from handcuffs.

The sheriff's deputy stated, "You'll need to accompany us to our office so you can give us a statement."

They both replied in unison. "Of course."

A deputy accompanied Jerk One in an ambulance. Another drove Jerk Two away.

The sheriff put them in his vehicle. After a bumpy

ride down the mountain they were again separated at the sheriff's office. The deputies proceeded to ask questions and have them write out their statements. It took longer than she'd expected. She saw Trevor leave the room across from where she sat long before she got released. As she made her way down the hall to the waiting room, she noticed Trevor pacing the floor.

When he spotted her he took three giant steps to reach her. "Madison, are you all right?"

"Lord, what an ordeal. It seemed more like an interrogation than a request for my statement." She took his proffered arm. As they strolled outside the building she saw the sun coming up.

"I could use a cup of coffee. How about you?"

"Absolutely," Madison replied.

"They said they'd take me to my car sometime later today. Did they offer you a ride back to your cabin?" Trevor asked as they strolled toward a café which appeared to be open.

"Yes, but not for a while. They plan to go over it and collect any forensics. I'm supposed to stick around town. Where do they think I'll go without any money or a vehicle?"

"At least I have my wallet. I sure hope this place has more than coffee. Even after the meal you fixed last night I'm still hungry." He opened the door and the aroma of bacon, coffee, and some kind of pastry wafted toward them.

"Heavens, it smells like my grandmother's kitchen." Madison slid into a booth.

There weren't many patrons, but they'd all stopped talking when she and Trevor entered. The waitress came over with menus and the crowd started talking again.

"Can I get you folks some coffee to start with?" The waitress pulled out her pad and pencil.

"Absolutely." Trevor gave her a smile that would melt any woman's heart. "I hope you have some big mugs or you'll be back here filling them up a lot."

When the waitress left, they perused their menus. It didn't take either of them more than a moment to decide what they wanted. They were ready to give the waitress their orders when she returned with their coffee.

She placed two large mugs on the table. "I hope this will hold you a few minutes. You folks the ones who took down those two bank robbers?"

Madison and Trevor looked at each other.

The waitress raised her eyebrows. "Small town. News travels fast."

"I don't think I'd use the words *take down,* but yeah, we caught 'em nappin'." Trevor grinned up at her. "Are we the topic of today's conversation?"

"Biggest news in years. Glad you didn't get hurt." She meandered back toward the kitchen and Madison noticed a lot of covert glances and hushed discussion aimed at them.

"Hmm, how long do you think it will be before someone else stops at the table and asks for more information?" Madison joked.

She noticed Trevor glancing over her shoulder when he mumbled, "Don't turn around…"

"I wanted to come by and shake your hand. I hear you young people are the ones who hogtied those two scum bags and held 'em for the sheriff."

"We didn't exactly hogtie them, but, yeah. Glad we could help," Trevor responded. Madison noticed Trevor's face turning red at the attention.

Before anyone else had a chance to stop by, the waitress came back with their food. "I'll make sure those busy-bodies don't bother you while you're eating. I'll be right back with more coffee."

Madison managed to suppress the giggle that almost erupted.

When the waitress returned Madison grinned. "Thanks for the coffee and everything else you're doing."

She waved in acknowledgement then wandered back to the counter. Madison took notice of Trevor's expression. He was having the same problem as she. She quickly stared at her plate so as not to break out in a full laugh. Busy putting her napkin in her lap and pepper on her eggs, she controlled her urges before taking another sip of coffee.

They ate in silence. By the end of their meal they'd managed to make eye contact without wanting to laugh.

"I think we better leave before we disgrace ourselves," Trevor suggested.

"Agreed." Not having any money Madison couldn't even leave the tip. She made a mental note of how much she owed Trevor. No need for him to foot the bill.

As they left the café they noticed more people coming in. It must be the town's gathering place.

"Let's head over to the grocery store and pick up the items we used at the cabin last night. I'm sure the owner will have enough problems repairing his front door where those jerks broke in."

"We ate the food, we should replace it. Since the

Jerks ate some of my food I'll need to replace that too. When I make it back to my cabin I want to pay my half of everything. I'm keeping track." She wanted Trevor to know her intentions.

He hesitated and then shrugged. "It goes against my upbringing to let a lady pay, but under the circumstances I understand why you want to."

"It's only fair. It's not like we're on a date."

"Does that mean you're going to help me chop some firewood to replace what we used?" he joked.

Laughing in spite of herself she replied, "I'll let the big, ripped hunk do it. Thank you very much."

"Big, ripped hunk?" It was Trevor's turn to laugh.

Her face grew warm at the slip. "Now don't let the compliment go to your head."

They both smiled as they entered the grocery store and picked up the few replacement items. One extra item they selected was a newspaper. No telling how long it would take for the sheriff to take them to Trevor's SUV.

Returning to the sheriff's office they settled into the most uncomfortable chairs Madison had sat in for some time. They each read the various sections of the newspaper.

Madison's mind drifted to Trevor while she pretended to read the paper. If she'd met him under different circumstances, she would have run the other way knowing he was in the army. She had no intentions of dating a soldier. After spending twenty-four hours with him under the strange situation they'd been in, she wouldn't have wanted anyone else to help extract her from the bank robbers turned kidnappers. So how would that translate to a relationship? Why contemplate a relationship with

Trevor? Must be his hot body.

Trying to switch her thoughts away from Trevor, she commented, “It’s good to be caught up on the news since I haven’t heard or read anything for days.” Madison put down the last portion of the newspaper.

“The same with me. How long have you been at the cabin?”

“Four days. I’ve got four more before my dad picks me up.”

“What are you doing with your time? Fishing, hunting, or just relaxing?”

“Writing. I sold my first book this summer and the publisher wants the second book of the series by Christmas.” Madison frowned at the reminder of her goal. With the loss of more than a day, would she be able to make the deadline?

“I’m impressed. I don’t know any authors. I guess I should say any *other* authors. You could use this adventure as a plot, couldn’t you?”

She grinned. “I suppose it could be turned into a book especially since the ending turned out so well. You won’t mind if I use you as a character in one of my books?”

Trevor’s eyebrows shot up to his hairline. “Me? Why would you want to put me in one of your books?”

“Are you kidding? You’re the perfect hero. Did I mention I write romance novels?” Her mind immediately pictured Trevor. In bed. With her. *Uh-oh. Stop thinking like that.*

“Romance novels?” He chuckled. “My mom and sister like to read those.”

He seemed to want to avoid the comment she made

about his being a hero. "So how long have you been up here by yourself?"

"A week so far, with one more to go." Trevor frowned after his response.

"So what are you doing? No, let me guess. Fishing?" Fishing was a safe topic.

Her comment made him smile.

"No fair, you saw the trout in the skillet."

With a tilt of her head, she grinned. "I admit it was a big clue."

"Yep. That and thinking. I came up here to work through some major stuff in my life."

She was startled by his candor. "I hope you've figured things out."

Surprise appeared on his face. "If you'd asked me yesterday I'd have said no. But now, I think I have."

"So our *adventure*, as you called it, has made things clear?" How interesting. Madison took in his shocked expression.

After several seconds he finally replied, "I think it has. Funny, isn't it?"

"I'm not sure I'd classify it as funny, but I'm glad it's helped."

"Me too." Trevor shook his head and rubbed his hand over his face.

Before they could continue their conversation Madison's satellite phone rang. "Uh-oh. Must be my dad." Madison glanced at her watch and noticed it was thirty minutes past the time slot for her promised call. "I'm late in calling. Excuse me."

"Hello, Dad." Madison did her best to sound cheerful

as she went outside to finish her conversation with her father. "Sorry I didn't call on schedule, but it's been a crazy twenty-four hours." Knowing the story would be all over the news she plunged in. "You may have heard about some bank robbers from Atlanta being caught here in the mountains."

"How did you know? I didn't think you had a TV or radio up there." Her father's comment sounded more like an accusation than a question.

Steeling herself for the barrage of questions, she told him how she'd spent the time since their last conversation.

CHAPTER FIVE

Trevor considered what he admitted to Madison while she took her phone call outside. Yes, the *adventure* had indeed made things clear. He'd been trying to determine if he should stay an active duty officer in the army or switch to the reserves. With an original eight-year commitment after his Reserve Officer Training Course in college he had four more years to go. When he started his army career he planned to work until retirement. After two deployments to the Middle East he'd become disillusioned with the army and its goals.

After tracking down the bank robbers who'd terrorized Madison and tried to kill them, he knew being a soldier was his calling. The skills he'd learned in the army made it possible for him to do what he'd accomplished yesterday. Those same skills helped people in other nations not as fortunate as people in the United States. Yes, the vision of his future became clear again. At least for his career. However, after meeting Madison, his personal life seemed more uncertain.

He'd been a confirmed bachelor for years and had no

intention of changing. Until he met Madison. She was the type of woman who made a man want to settle down. Her strength and courage during their time together had impressed him. After today he'd probably never see her again. No, he'd make sure he did.

Madison came back inside with an air of frustration surrounding her.

"From your expression I gather your father is upset about what happened."

"Upset is an understatement. He probably has the sheriff on the phone right now. I hope you don't mind, but I gave him your name. He wants to make sure you aren't an axe murderer or something." She plopped down in the chair across from him.

He chuckled. "He wouldn't be a good father if he didn't. Of course, if I had been an axe murderer, I think I missed my best opportunity."

Madison gave him a wry smile. "I decided it best not to mention it."

"Can't blame you."

If she didn't live too far away he'd ask her for a date. "So where do you live when you aren't cloistered away writing?"

"Macon, Georgia."

"That's not too far from Columbus."

"True."

He liked the idea it wouldn't be too difficult to arrange another meeting. "So do you have a full time job in addition to your writing?"

"For now I teach high school English. Someday I'd like to devote all my time to writing."

Trevor didn't think he'd had a teacher as attractive as Madison. "Perfect job for a writer, I'd think. You have summers off to write."

"Exactly what I've been doing since I graduated. Of course, I write during the school year as well, but not as much."

"Where did you go to college?" He surprised himself with his curiosity. He couldn't stop questioning Madison.

"Wesleyan. It's a woman's college in Macon."

"Yeah, I've heard of it. It's where all the rich, fancy girls go, right?"

She frowned. "No, not everyone is rich. It has an excellent reputation with a great curriculum." Her answer came out in a sharp tone.

"Sorry. I didn't mean any disrespect." He recognized a riled female when he heard one. "I've heard they have a great graduation rate." He hoped it was true and removed his foot from his mouth.

"Yes, they do." She shifted in her chair and crossed her arms. "So where did you attend?"

He figured her pause indicated she was trying not to be pissed off.

"Texas A&M."

"Ah, and you went through their ROTC deparment, right?" Plenty of cadets earned their way through college through the reserve officer training program.

"Yep, it helped pay for college and gave me a job when I graduated. It seemed like a good plan." His family didn't have a lot of money, so paying for college had all been on him.

"How much longer will you be stationed at Fort

Benning?"

He shrugged his shoulders. "It depends."

He noticed Madison's perplexed expression before she said, "Doesn't it always?"

"If your dad was in the army I guess you know how it works."

Since she'd grown up as a military brat she'd know how transfers and deployments occurred.

"Guess I do. When did you return from deployment?"

Acknowledging her astute observation he replied, "Obvious, huh? About a month ago."

"To people who are familiar, yes it is," she agreed. "Then you shouldn't have to deploy again for a while."

"Not likely." With his specialized unit he never knew for sure.

"Does it have something to do with why you're up here?"

He knew she understood. "Exactly. I've been trying to decide whether I'm going to stay active duty or go reserve."

Cocking her head to the side, she studied him for a moment. "Have you made a decision yet?"

"Actually, I have. My original plan was to be a lifer. For a lot of reasons I recently questioned my decision. After taking time to consider everything I'm going to stick with the plan." He wanted to be upfront about his future. If they pursued a relationship he wanted no doubt about his desire for an army career.

"Glad you've come to a decision. I'm sure it wasn't easy." Madison gave him a sad smile.

Before Trevor could ask another question, the deputy

came out of the office. "All right, folks, we can take you back to your cabins now."

Trevor and Madison gathered up the few bags of groceries and followed the deputy out to the parking lot. The deputy talked nonstop as they headed to the cabin where they'd left Trevor's SUV. "I hope those guys don't get out on bail. That one fella sure has it in for you, Ms. Hendricks."

"He said something to me a few minutes before you arrived. Do you think he's serious?"

"Never can tell with men like him. They come up with a crazy idea and it turns into a mission. They can't never admit anything is their fault."

Trevor patted Madison on the shoulder. "Don't worry. He'll have me to deal with if he does."

Madison smiled and said nothing.

Upon their arrival the deputy turned to Madison. "I can drive you up to your cabin if you want."

"No need. I'll put these groceries away while Trevor chops some wood. When we're done he'll take me to my cabin."

"I'll have to open the door for you and wait. We've nailed it shut until the owner arrives. He's been notified of the break-in."

"Oh, well, I'll be quick, but I'll wait here until Trevor is finished."

Trevor went out to the backyard to chop wood. He took off his jacket before starting his chore. A few minutes later he took off his long-sleeved shirt with only a short-sleeved T-shirt covering his chest. Madison soon appeared around the corner and strode over to watch him work.

Although he hadn't considered his movements, he couldn't help notice Madison's admiring glance. His T-shirt fitted tight and he knew his years of field training had given him a muscular physique.

"How far is it from Macon to Columbus?" Trevor swung the axe, splitting the wood into pieces the right size for the fireplace.

"It's right around one hundred miles and takes a little under two hours. Why?"

He noticed an edge to her voice. He stopped chopping long enough to watch her expression while he said, "If you don't object I'd like to drive over and take you to dinner." He could tell she'd turn him down if he didn't give her a reason. Other than the obvious one, asking her for a date. "A thank-you dinner for feeding me last night. If it hadn't been for your cooking I might have passed out from hunger."

Her laugh made him hopeful. She glared at him with narrowed eyes. "So you aren't asking me for a date, right?"

"Why would I do that?" His best innocent expression had fooled more than one mother of a girl he'd dated. "It's a simple thank you."

She paused quite a while before responding. "I can't believe I'm saying this, but sure. Why not? Of course, I have more cause to say thank you to you than you have a reason to thank me."

"So then you can take me to dinner another time. Deal?" Again, he gave her his best innocent look knowing she'd seen right through him.

She rolled her eyes and smiled. "I know I'm going to regret this, but I'll leave it at maybe. No promises."

Nodding, he went back to chopping kindling. He had his work cut out for him. If her father was retired army and planned to check up on him, perhaps he'd do the same. It could work in his favor if he managed things the right way.

When he had enough firewood to replace what they used he put the axe back where he found it. "How about giving me a hand? There's a spot outside the kitchen door to stack this." With an armload of wood he led the way.

"Sure." Madison picked up a few pieces and followed Trevor. A couple more trips each and they had a neat stack next to the back door.

"Guess it's time to take you up to your cabin." Trevor walked next to Madison and they climbed into his SUV. He made sure to switch the anti-theft lever so the vehicle wouldn't stop dead in its tracks in a mile.

"Thanks for everything, Trevor." Her sincerity humbled him. "I'm sure I'd be dead if anyone but you had answered the door."

"Don't underestimate yourself. You did a good job of saving your own bacon," he commented, trying to deflect her praise.

"I won't argue that I tried."

She seemed to want to say more, but for some reason stopped. Good. He hated to be complimented on mere instinct.

He pulled up in front of the cabin she'd rented. "Wait here. I'll go inside and make sure you didn't have some animal scurry in there while you were gone."

She seemed startled at his comment. "Oh, lord, I hadn't even thought about that. If there's a skunk in there I may have to cancel the rest of my vacation." She laughed at her own joke.

"Now I'll tread even more carefully." He opened the front door with caution. He grabbed the fireplace poker to jab into the corners of the closets and under the bed to make sure some small creature hadn't taken up residence.

When he stepped into the bathroom he noticed a pair of red lace panties and matching bra hanging from the shower rod. The panties wouldn't cover much. He groaned as his active imagination went into overdrive. Madison, wearing those scraps of material, leaving little to guess at what lay beneath. Good God, how would he put those visions out of his head? He closed his eyes and drew in the fragrance she wore. Backing out of the bathroom, he stood for a moment trying to compose his wild thoughts and struggled to keep his arousal from becoming too apparent. He went to the kitchen sink and turned on the cold water to splash on his face.

Trying to replace his vision of Madison, he mentally broke down his rifle and put it back together. There. All under control.

He strode back to the front porch where Madison sat rocking in one of the two chairs. "All clear. No large or small animals roaming through your space."

"I figured you found something. You were in there so long."

"Trying to be thorough. I'll let you return to your writing." He started down the steps toward his SUV. "Oh, I almost forgot to get your number." He stared at her expectantly.

"Let me find a slip of paper and write it down for you." She stood up and started toward the door.

“No need. Rattle it off and I’ll remember.”

Madison’s eyebrows rose at his comment, but she gave him her digits.

“I’ll call you and set up a time for our dinner.” He waved goodbye and climbed back into his SUV and drove to his cabin.

He needed the casual departure to keep her suspicions about his feelings under control. Wooing Madison would take determination and stealth.

CHAPTER SIX

Madison wandered into the cabin checking for evidence of the invasion. To her surprise the only major reminder resided in the kitchen. The robbers had raided her food supply and cracker crumbs, eggs shells, and coffee grounds littered the counter and table. She made a pot of coffee. Eyes open for more than twenty-four hours, it would be the only thing keeping her awake. As she tidied up the mess she forced her mind back to her book. Having lost over a day of writing time she needed to concentrate more than ever to complete as much as possible during her holiday to meet her deadline.

A shower would help her wake up and heaven knew she needed one. She came to an abrupt halt as she strode into the bathroom. "Oh, lord, I'd forgotten about those." She plucked her undergarments down from the shower rod. "I'll bet a dollar Trevor enjoyed this when he cleared the cabin." She groaned as she put them away in the dresser. "Now he knows my secret indulgence." Taking a moment to deal with the sudden hot desire to wear nothing but sexy lingerie for Trevor, she acknowledged her increased craving for his touch.

Madison shucked off her clothes and stepped into a cold shower. The shock cooled her ardor and she forced her mind to the unfinished manuscript. Finishing up quickly, she dried off and pulled on a new set of jeans and long-sleeved sweater.

Drawing out her laptop from the nightstand where she'd set it up to recharge while she'd taken her early morning constitutional the day before, she admitted the events following her walk had changed her life. The last several hours had been the most adrenaline pumping adventure of her life. Now she had to return to routine work. Forcing her mind back to the task at hand she realized her book's hero matched Trevor's appearance. Smiling at the coincidence, she considered asking him to pose for the cover art. Laughing out loud at the idea, she arranged her work at the kitchen table and plunged into writing.

Although the first hour she struggled to get back into the writing zone, she finally managed to make progress. After hours of typing, she acknowledged the growls her stomach made and stopped for food. Reviewing her options, it dawned on her she'd never had lunch and it was almost five o'clock. Might as well make dinner. Smiling about the high praise Trevor had given her mac-n-cheese, she made it again. Note to self – walk an extra mile to make up for it.

As she busied herself with the task her mind drifted to Trevor. If only he wasn't in the army. She'd promised herself she would never marry or even date a soldier. Her experience as a military brat taught her a soldier's time away from home was stressful on the family, never knowing if they would return or if they did if they would be whole. Her best friend's father came home minus a leg and an arm. He'd been so angry he made her friend and mother cry; they were terrified to do anything to upset him.

Trevor's good looks and personality couldn't overcome the fact he planned to be a career soldier. Might as well not think about him. There. That's settled.

Eating her solitary dinner, Madison admitted she'd told herself the biggest lie ever.

Returning to her manuscript, she kept at it until ten o'clock. She stood up, stretched, and then did some exercises she'd learned to release the built up tension in her shoulders and back created from all the typing. As she contemplated having a glass of milk and a granola bar her satellite phone rang.

"Hey, baby girl, how you doin'?"

"Hi, Dad. I'm fine. We weren't due for another call until morning."

"I know. After what you told me about the day you had I wanted to check to make sure you were okay staying alone. What time did you return to the cabin?"

"Close to one o'clock this afternoon."

"Do you want me to drive by tomorrow to pick you up? Will you be all right by yourself?"

"Thanks, Dad. I appreciate you thinking about me, but I still have a deadline. I can't afford to mess up this opportunity."

"Somehow I knew you'd say that. I could come stay with you to make sure you're safe. I'll go fishing or hunting so I won't disturb you."

"Again, thank you for the offer. I'm fine. I'm going to sleep and jump back into writing first thing in the morning. Thanks for checking on me."

"It's what I live for. Good night, sweetheart."

"Good night, Dad."

When she turned off the phone the comment her father had made about what he lived for struck her as poignant. It was a phrase he used often since her mother died, but the meaning had never sunk in until now. Her father did live for doing all the right things for her. And for their country. Why had it taken so long for her to understand?

Preparing for bed her visions of Trevor returned. No. She couldn't let that happen. She'd never manage to sleep. Forcing her mind back to her book, exhaustion from being up so many hours caused her to fall asleep the moment her head hit the pillow.

Shortly before dawn she woke. She'd been dreaming of Trevor in her bed back in Macon. With her. Naked. Making love. Knowing sleep would continue to elude her, she got up and put on a pot of coffee. After a quick shower and even quicker breakfast, she slipped on her jacket. She put the phone in one pocket, then picked up her cup and left for her morning stroll.

Today her feet headed toward Trevor's cabin. She knew it was a bad idea, but couldn't stop her need to see him again. Arriving at a boat dock next to his cabin she made herself comfortable in one of the Adirondack chairs. She sipped her coffee. If Trevor didn't make an appearance by the time she finished, she'd leave.

Not sure if she was pleased or not, Trevor exited his

cabin whistling as he made his way toward her.

"You surprised me when I spotted you a few minutes ago. How long have you been here?" He sat in the chair across from her.

Madison grinned. "Not long. I know it's early, but as a fisherman I figured you'd be up by now."

"Being a fisherman has nothing to do with it. I've always been an early riser. How's your book coming along?" He relaxed in the chair. His eyes never wavered from her face.

She struggled not to squirm under his scrutiny. "I made a lot of progress yesterday. Still behind schedule after everything." She waved her hand toward his cabin to indicate the events of the previous two days.

"Sorry to hear it," he answered with an impassive face. "So why aren't you back at it?"

"I have to take a break now and again." She shrugged. "I start out each morning with a walk to energize me for the day. It also allows me time to work out the scenes I plan to write next."

"So you decided to come this direction today?" The tilt of his head made it seem like he thought there might be more to it than routine. He was right, damn it.

Not that she'd tell him that. "Exactly. I haven't taken this path yet. When I came down the other day we took the road. This is more direct, but Jerk One and Two didn't know any other way."

He crossed his legs. "I'm glad you stopped by. Would you like to go fishing with me?"

"Thanks for the offer. I do enjoy casting a line on occasion, but as I mentioned I'm behind schedule."

Madison stood up to make her exit.

He touched her arm to draw her attention. "Would you like a refill of coffee before you go?"

"Do you have some already made?"

"Yes, I do. I plan to take a thermos out with me, but I know there will be at least another cup in the pot if you want it."

"Thanks. I won't turn down coffee."

Once back inside, Trevor pointed to the full coffee pot. "Go ahead and fix your cup then I'll fill the thermos."

"You haven't had any yet?" She couldn't hide her astonishment.

He chuckled. "Actually, this is the second pot. I've been up for a while."

She grinned. "A man after my own heart. I think I could drink coffee all day."

"Normally one pot is enough, but my clock is a bit off kilter after the extra long day we had."

"I know what you mean. Well, thanks for the refill." She put the top back on her cup. "I better return to work and let you continue your fishing."

Madison strolled toward the back door and reached out to the grab the knob.

"One more thing before you go."

Madison spun to find Trevor inches from her. He took her coffee cup and set it on the window sill within reach. Before she had any idea what he planned to do, he took her in his arms and kissed her. She instinctively wrapped her arms around his neck and melted into him. He tasted of coffee and smelled of the outdoors. The kiss started out light and probing. When she opened her mouth to take in more, he plunged his tongue deep and ran his hand up and down her back.

Loving the feel of him she tried to push closer. Trevor's arousal caused a chain reaction in her nether regions, soaking her panties. Much too soon he released her and stepped back.

Off balance, she stared at him. "Why did you stop?"

"You need to go back to your writing." He gave her a sad smile. "I figured if I didn't stop now I might not let you go."

"Oh," was all she could think to say as she blinked at him. She turned and grabbed her cup. "Thanks for the coffee." She made her way out the door and back toward her cabin. So what did that mean? Her reaction had been purely physical. She couldn't deny Trevor's sex appeal. And she'd been writing a romance novel with a hero who had all his traits. Natural reaction. Nothing more. Right. Lying to herself had become a habit of late.

Before she knew it her cabin came into view. She wandered in and sat down at the kitchen table, full coffee cup in hand. Realizing coffee was available she took a slug. He made good coffee. Another point in his favor. He didn't need anymore, she lectured.

After sitting in stunned silence for a moment she quit thinking about him and got back to work. At this rate she wouldn't finish her first draft. Then where would she be?

Setting up her laptop, she did her best to erase thoughts of Trevor from her mind long enough to become immersed in her writing. Things went well for an hour or so. Then she came to the love scene for her book. She immediately pictured Trevor like she'd seen in her dream.

In her bed. With her. Deciding to go with it, she wrote the scene as it played out once again in her mind. After she'd put the words on paper she was certain it was time for a break. Good thing she finished the love scene otherwise she'd need a cold shower. Standing and stretching she glanced at the clock. Good. Only nine o'clock. Checking her word count she felt elated for meeting her goal for the morning and three more hours to write until lunch. After completing a few exercises and switching to a glass of iced tea, she sat back down for more work.

Around one o'clock she stopped long enough for a short lunch break. She worked until seven in the evening. Her stomach growled, reminding her it was time for dinner. She needed something more substantial than a sandwich. Reviewing her options, she selected grilled chicken, roasted okra, and some sliced tomatoes. Deciding not to cook outside, which would attract animals, she used the indoor grill. In no time her meal was ready and she sat at the table. Having had enough silence for the day she pulled out an iPod and selected some oldies music. It reminded her of her childhood when she and her mother were alone waiting for her father's return from some mission. Her mother taught her how to dance to the sixties music which she learned from her mother. The memories of fun times made her smile.

Working a few more hours after dinner she was satisfied with her progress. One more day at this pace and she'd make up the time she'd lost. The first draft would be finished. Editing would come next, but she'd be back at school by then.

Once again, she fell asleep the minute her head hit

the pillow.

Writing, writing, writing. She only stopped for meals and her morning stroll until the last day of her vacation dawned. Her final task came down to packing then waiting for her father to arrive around noon for a ride back home. Her determination had kept her from thinking too much about Trevor and the kiss they'd shared. Would he call like he'd promised? What if he didn't? Images of what could be kept pushing into her thoughts.

Finishing her second cup she meandered down to Trevor's cabin. Before she knew it she stood on the dock. The boat rocked gently next to it so there was a good chance Trevor was still in the cabin. Unless he was out hunting. She'd heard some gunshots the day before which triggered memories of the shoot out at Trevor's cabin. The shots made her realize he must have switched from fishing to hunting.

Deciding to wait a while before knocking on his door, she sat down in the same Adirondack chair she used a couple of days ago. In no time she spotted Trevor leaving his cabin and wandering in her direction.

"I hoped you'd stop by before you left. This is the day you head back home, right?"

"Yep, this is the day. My dad will be by around noon. I wanted to say good-bye."

"I wondered if I'd scared you off with our kiss."

Sighing as if it meant nothing, Madison said, "It was unexpected. I also wanted to make you aware I don't date military men. Ever. So if we go out to dinner, it's as friends. That's all."

A frown formed on his face. "Why don't you go out

with men in the miliary?"

Although it took effort, she looked him in the eye when she told him. "Having been an army brat, I won't take a chance it would turn into something more. Understand?" To cement the understanding she stuck out her hand in order to shake his.

Trevor took her hand and drew her close, then placed her arm around his waist. His intent obvious. He slowly placed his lips lightly on hers. Not pressuring her to respond, he held them there a few moments before taking his tongue and tracing her lips. Shivering with want she stepped back.

"I'll settle for friendship. For now."

"I mean it, Trevor, our relationship won't go beyond what we have now."

"I've never known anyone to have too many friends."

Before she could analyze his comment he continued. "When your dad picks you up why don't you stop by on your way back down the mountain? I can have lunch ready. Rainbow trout, right out of the river."

Her father adored fresh trout, so she agreed. "Thanks. Nice of you to share your catch. We'll see you shortly after noon."

What had just happened? Stunned, she made her way back to the cabin. Had she been outmaneuvered?

CHAPTER SEVEN

Grinning at his cleverly finessed plan to meet Madison's father, Trevor made his way back inside. By now her father would have checked him out. He felt certain he would pass with flying colors. As a retired soldier, he knew Madison's dad would approve of her dating an army officer.

Grabbing his fishing pole, he figured he better catch a couple more trout to make sure there would be plenty for lunch. Whistling as he made his way toward the dock, he considered his plan. Win over the father, the daughter would follow.

Shortly before noon Trevor sat on the front porch to watch for a vehicle. He didn't know if her father had been enlisted or officer, but it didn't matter. Not to him. He'd know the minute the man entered the cabin. As he spotted an SUV traveling north, he knew before seeing the army stickers on the window it was Madison's father. There was only one cabin north and only one person who would be driving there today.

He already had a can of corn warming on the stove

and the fish were skinned and filleted. Once he heard the car pulling to a stop in his yard, he started frying the fish.

"Come on in," he said in response to the knock at his door. "Welcome to the woods." Trevor grinned and strode up to Madison's father with his hand out. "Thanks for stopping by. I'm Trevor Montgomery."

Madison's father shook his hand. "Ashton Hendricks. Thanks for the invitation. I planned to stop by to thank you for what you did the other night. The sheriff told me more of the story than Madison did." He glanced in her direction.

"Now, Dad—"

Her father waved his hand in dismissal. "I know, I know. You didn't want to worry me. Things turned out all right so I won't pester you about it."

"I'm sure anyone would have done the same thing in the circumstances, sir." Trevor knew from the man's stance, direct eye contact, and voice, he'd been an officer. Calling him *sir* came automatically.

"They might have wanted to, but I doubt many men could have tracked down those scumbags the way you did. The sheriff was surprised you managed to get the drop on those two guys."

"I need to turn the fish before they burn." Trevor marched back into the kitchen area. The cabin contained only three rooms so the kitchen lay a mere five steps away. "That was the easy part. They slept like the dead. The satellite phone you gave Madison made the biggest difference. It kept us from driving those guys to town and searching for the sheriff's office. No telling what could have happened if we'd had to."

"When she told me of her plans to be up here where

cell phone service is nonexistant and refusing to take a gun, I insisted she at least take the phone. Glad to hear it came in handy for more than a daily chat."

"Dad, I already thanked you." Madison turned pink.

"I know you did, sweetheart. Glad to have someone else recognize a father's need to keep his daughter safe."

Trevor refrained from commenting since Madison seemed put-out at the idea. "Lunch is ready. Go ahead and sit down." He put a plate containing two huge fillets at each chair. Two separate bowls held a salad and corn. "I hope you like ranch dressing, it's the only variety I have."

"I'm surprised you have fresh greens." Madison sat at the small table.

Caught in the act, he confessed. "I have to admit I drove to the store earlier. I figured you'd want something more than the fish."

She laughed at his disclosure. "Thank you for the consideration. I haven't had a fresh salad in days and I do appreciate it."

Trevor directed a question to Madison's father. "I understand you've retired from the army. What are you doing now?"

"Since my retirement after Madison graduated from college I stuck around Columbus as a consultant to the army."

"So I might see you around base."

"Yes, that's a possibility."

Chatting about inconsequential things during lunch, Trevor knew he'd made a good impression on Madison's father. He smiled and waved as they drove down the mountain. Having refused their offer to clean up the lunch plates, he busied himself with the task. Now that he had an ally, he felt sure he'd see more of Madison in the near future.

After returning to Ft. Benning, he met with his superiors and announced his decision to continue as an active duty soldier. Once finished with the paperwork, he called his family to let them know of his decision.

"Well, son. You know we're proud of you."

"Thanks, Dad."

"It's still difficult to know when you're deployed to the Middle East or some other godforsaken place where you're in harms way."

"I know it must be hard on you and Mom. It's what I do and who I am."

"Yeah, son, it is. We pray for you."

"Thanks. I'm always grateful."

His awareness of his parents concern also cemented his view that men in his position shouldn't marry. The idea that a wife and maybe a child or two who were dependent on him would be left without resources in the event of his death wasn't right. Most of his fellow rangers were single. Those who were married had problems with their relationships. The life they led seemed to ensure it.

So maybe he shouldn't call Madison for dinner. No matter how attracted he was to her.

CHAPTER EIGHT

Despite his decision, he couldn't get her off his mind. Each night he dreamed of her and their meetings ended with the two of them in bed among a tangle of sheets. He decided seeing her one more time would make her less of a fantasy, get her out of his system. Picking up the phone he dialed her number.

"It's about time you called."

Trevor blinked at Madison's response. "I guess my plan worked. You missed me."

"Oh, ah, Trevor. I thought you were someone else."

"Now you've hurt my feelings." He didn't give her time to reply as he rushed on. "You can make it up to me. Have dinner with me Thursday night."

"Thursday?" she said in a slow drawl.

He figured she must be thinking of an excuse not to accept. "Exactly. Date nights are Friday or Saturday. Thursdays are set aside for friends, so you're safe."

Her long pause caused him to think she wouldn't accept.

"You're in luck. I don't have plans for Thursday.

Want to meet some place between here and Ft. Benning?"

"If we do, then you'll have to drive home after dark. My mama would take a switch to me if I let a single female drive home on a lonely road at night. I'll come to Macon." He wouldn't consider another option.

She laughed. "I wouldn't want your mother to go to the trouble. All right. Let me think of some options."

"Great. I'll leave right after work so I can pick you up around six-thirty. Is that okay?"

"Yes. Dress casual. Since it's not a date, neither of us have to dress up. Right?"

"You know it." Trevor disconnected their call. Pleased at his success he popped open a beer in celebration.

CHAPTER NINE

Thursday arrived and Madison felt foolish as she picked through her entire closet selecting something to wear. Choosing the right thing for a casual non-date turned out to be much more difficult than she expected. Moments after she finished dressing the doorbell rang. Glancing at her watch she smiled. Leave it to a military man to arrive exactly at the appointed time.

"Trevor. Good to see you." Madison gave him a kiss on the cheek. "Come on in. All I need is my coat and I'm ready." Madison turned to take two short steps to her coat closet.

"It was worth the drive for your kiss."

She chuckled. "You are easy to satisfy if a peck on the cheek can bring you a hundred miles." Madison handed him her coat and he helped her slip it on.

"No way can I respond to such a comment without causing harm to my macho status."

"Uh-oh. I didn't think…" Had she stepped on his ego? His easy grin made her relax.

"Exactly. So let's drop it and head out to the car.

Where are we going?"

"There's this great steak place…"

They continued to the restaurant where they chatted, drank wine, and enjoyed each other's company. Madison felt more relaxed with Trevor than any other man she'd dated. Maybe because this didn't qualify as a date. But he was comfortable to talk to and be around. Be herself.

As Trevor drove them back to her house she asked, "I know you had some wine with dinner. Would you like a cup of coffee to help you stay awake on the drive home?"

"Sounds like a great idea, if you don't mind."

"Of course not. That's why I asked. Come on in and I'll make a pot. We can chat a while longer with a cup then I'll fix you one to take with you."

"Perfect."

They talked and drank coffee for thirty minutes before Trevor stood up. "I need to head back. I'm glad you let me take you to dinner."

"And I'm glad you convinced me. I had a great time."

"So, I can call again?"

Madison hesitated. "Do you think it's a good idea?"

"Why not? We're just friends. Right?"

"Right."

"Okay. Then give me a cup of coffee for the road and a good-night kiss and I'll be on the road."

"A good-night kiss?"

"Hey, is it asking too much? From a friend?"

Madison gave him a look she knew conveyed her doubt. "All right. Only a friendly kiss."

"I'll take it." Trevor leaned over and gave her a

chaste kiss on the lips. For some reason she felt disappointed.

CHAPTER TEN

Trevor smiled as he drove out of Macon. He'd wanted to give her more than the peck at the end of the evening, but knew she'd never agree to see him again if he did. His smile faded as he considered his intentions.

His plan to make her less of a fantasy backfired. He wanted her more than ever. He knew she didn't date military men. She'd been adamant. Could he change her mind? Had he changed his about marriage?

Not knowing the answers, Trevor continued their friendship and called for a non-date every couple of weeks then increased their meetings to weekly. He never asked for a Friday or Saturday. Sometimes they went to dinner, sometimes to a movie. Then he started cooking for her. He'd bring the ingredients and they cooked in her kitchen. Each time he said good night their friendly kiss lasted a little longer. He pulled her close when they watched a movie. The first time she'd stiffened then relaxed. Now she melted into him.

Christmas arrived and he went home to Texas for a week. As soon as he returned, he called Madison to suggest they stay at her place and cook. "I make the best shrimp and grits you've ever put in your mouth."

"Since I've never eaten shrimp and grits, I'm sure you're right."

"What? I can't believe you've lived in the South and not eaten shrimp and grits."

"I admit I'm not a big fan of grits."

"I'll fix that. Wait and see."

Madison's tinkling laugh caused a surge of desire.

"You're on." Even to his own ears his voice sounded lower and gravelly. Would it scare her away?

When Tuesday arrived he showed up at six o'clock and knocked on Madison's door. He'd left work early to extend their time together. His fellow rangers noted his early departures and ribbed him about it and tried to pry Madison's name out of him. Not yet. He didn't want to say her name to anyone else in case it might jinx their relationship.

Madison opened the door. "Come in. How was Christmas with your family?"

"Fantastic. Always good to see everyone. I think I gained twenty pounds."

"Some of my students brought me homemade goodies. I had to share with my family to avoid eating it all myself. Even then I'm scared to step on the scales."

"Did you finish the edits for your book on schedule?"

"Yes, I did. In fact I emailed it two days early. Now I've started on book three of the series."

They moved into the kitchen and unloaded the grocery bags Trevor brought with him.

"Good idea to take advantage of your time off."

They pulled out pots and pans.

"Exactly. School starts again in a few days so I'm trying to write as much as I can. Changing the subject, how about next time we try cooking lamb?"

Trevor stopped pulling items out of the grocery bag then turned to face Madison. "Lamb?"

She spun toward him and put a hand on her hip. "I love the way Mediterranian dishes are seasoned. Especially lamb. Are you game?"

"Sure. I'll see if I can find someone who can give us some tips."

"Do you mind if I turn on the news? I've been deep in my book and haven't taken time to find out what is happening."

"Go ahead."

They continued cooking and listened to the news. As they took their plates to the table a breaking news story caught their attention.

"WMAZ-TV brings you a Special Report. Two men arrested in October for the armed robbery of The First Bank of East Georgia in Atlanta have escaped Gwinnet County Jail. As they were transported yesterday afternoon to the courthouse for pretrial motions their vehicle collided with a garbage truck. Officials explained that during the confusion after the crash they managed to elude police."

A phone number scrolled across the screen listing who to call to report information leading to their arrest.

"Oh, lord. They have to be Jerk One and Jerk Two." Madison placed her plate on the table.

Trevor motioned with his plate toward her set. "I can't believe they put that information on television."

Turning back to watch the TV, Madison saw additional details scroll across. “Why would they put my name and the school where I work?”

“You’re the person they kidnapped after the robbery. Sensationalism. The station has no idea the danger they put you in.” Trevor placed his plate and salad bowl next to hers. He turned her towards him, put both hands on her upper arms, then stared into her eyes. “You need to be careful. Keep your doors and windows locked. Don’t go outside after dark without someone with you.”

Madison’s brow knitted. “What? Why?”

“They might come after you.”

She broke contact, turned off the television, and sat down at the dining table. “Come after me? He made that threat months ago.”

“He blames you for their capture.” Trevor took his seat and picked up his fork.

“I’d think they’d be more interested in leaving the country than tracking me down.”

His frown deepened. “I’d like to think you’re right, but it’s better to be cautious. Remember what that deputy said about men like that? They have a crazy idea and then it becomes their mission.”

“Hmm. He did. What about you?” Madison loaded her fork with a plump shrimp and creamy grits.

“They wouldn’t come after me.”

Madison’s eyebrows shot up. “Oh, and why not?” She took a mouthful, chewed, swallowed, and then paused and stared at her plate. “You’re right. I do like shrimp and grits.”

“Told ya. Sorry about the earlier comment. It

sounded a bit chauvinistic, didn't it." He took a bite.

"Ya think?"

"Be logical." He waved his empty fork for emphasis. "They don't know enough about me. If they found out and planned to come after me it would be on an army post. Lots of men and women with guns, not just me. Unfortunately, now they have enough details about you to track you down. Please promise you'll be careful. Maybe check in with someone every morning and again in the evening."

"I still don't know why'd they do it. Checking in twice a day is overly dramatic. I'll be fine." Madison ended the discussion with a chopping motion of her hand.

"They might want to intimidate you so you won't testify against them."

"But you would still testify. Right?"

Trevor shrugged. "If they threatened to do something to you I might back down."

Before she had a chance to reply, Madison's phone rang. She checked the caller ID as she answered. "Hi, Dad. What's up?" She rolled her eyes at Trevor.

After listening for several seconds, she said, "Not you too?" She paused and put one hand on her hip. "Trevor said the same thing. You are both overreacting. Those men are probably already in Mexico." Madison pressed a button on her phone. "Yes, Dad, Trevor is here with me. I put you on speaker phone." Her body language shouted her frustration.

"Hello, Trevor. I feel better knowing you are there with Madison right now."

"Hello, sir. Good to hear from you." He grinned at Madison, which caused her to roll her eyes again.

"Try to talk some sense into my girl, will you?"

"I asked her to check in twice a day with someone. I'm sure you'll agree."

"Yes, yes. She can call me each morning like she did when she was at the cabin. Good idea. You'll make an old man happy if you do, sweetheart."

Madison rolled her eyes and threw up her hands. "All right. All right. I can't battle two of you. Dad, I'll call you in the morning and Trevor, I'll call you around six in the evening. Will that keep the two of you off my back?"

"Yes." Both men announced.

They spoke a few more minutes and disconnected the call.

Finishing their cold dinner Trevor helped clean up the kitchen. He took a final swipe on the counter. "I'll be heading out. I know you want to work on your book."

"Thanks, Trevor. Yes, I do. I need to write as much as possible during this break."

"Call me tomorrow." He shook a finger at her.

She gave a single jerk of her head. "I'll set the alarm on my phone. Sheesh. You'd think I was sixteen again."

"Come give me a hug." He held out his arms and grinned at her.

Madison walked into them as she gave him a reluctant smile. "Thanks. I know you mean well."

"Yes, I do." Trevor didn't ask, but bent his head and covered her mouth with his.

This time he kissed her for real. No friendly peck. She tasted of bacon, grits, and shrimp. He drew her closer and she wrapped her arms around him. Trevor broke their kiss before allowing too much of his feelings to pour out.

She stumbled back and blinked several times."Wow. I mean, I think you need to leave."

"I will." He wanted to explain, but decided she needed time to consider the kiss. If he pushed now she'd respond without thinking. Time to retreat and regroup. "Talk to you tomorrow." He grabbed his coat and left.

He hoped the kiss showed her he didn't think of the two of them as merely friends. Did she feel the same way?

CHAPTER ELEVEN

Trevor hoped he hadn't spooked her with the good-night kiss. Their discussion about the bank robbers and his worry for her made him rash. He wanted to show her what she meant to him. Taking things slow had always been his plan. When she opened her mouth to his, he couldn't hold back. Stepping away from her cost him a few more moments of delight, but he didn't want her to notice his physical reaction. He strode out the door before putting on his coat. The chilled air helped cool his ardor.

The next evening, true to her word, Madison called at six o'clock.

"How did your writing go?"

"Pretty well. I set a goal for each day. I haven't reached today's word count so I need to get back at it. Hope you don't mind. Bye." She hung up.

He grinned. At least she called. As an optimist he took it as a good omen.

Each day went by much the same way for the next three days. A short call from Madison. Nothing personal discussed. On day four he sat at his kitchen table waiting for her call. Six-thirty came and went. Nothing. He called her cell and it went directly to voice mail. He called her father.

"Excuse me, sir, did you hear from Madison this morning?"

"Yes, I did."

"Did she sound okay?"

"Of course. Are you telling me you haven't heard from her this evening?"

"No, I haven't."

"Oh, lord. Please don't tell me we were right?"

"Call the Macon police. I'll come by and pick you up and we'll go to her house. Call Joan and ask her to contact their friends. See if any of them know where she is."

Trevor gathered guns, ammo, and a few other items before racing out the door. He had never been to the retired lieutenant colonel's house, but knew the general area. He spotted a man at the curb waving a flashlight. It had to be him.

Ashton Hendricks pulled the door open to Trevor's car before it managed to completely stop. "Let's go. I've been on the phone to all the friends I know. None of them have talked to her today. They knew she was writing so didn't think it unusual. Good thing we made her check with us, otherwise no one would have noticed."

"Did you call the police?"

"Yes, damn them. They agreed to do what they call a wellness check, nothing else. She's an adult and doesn't have to explain where she is. They won't do anything for at least twenty-four hours. Unless they see signs of foul play they may not do anything then."

Trevor hit his fist on the steering wheel as they raced to Macon. He made the two-hour trip in slightly over one. Joan contacted Ashton to report none of Madison's friends knew where she was. The men sat in silence. When they pulled into her drive two policemen sauntered down the sidewalk.

"Did you find anything, officer?" Ashton stepped out of the car.

"I'm sorry, sir, who are you?"

"The father of the woman who lives here. I'm the one who called. Did she answer the door?"

"No, she didn't. We checked out back and peered through the windows. We didn't see anything unusual. Do you have a key?"

"Yes, let's go inside and search for clues."

"You're certain she didn't leave with a friend? Her car is in the garage."

"I contacted her best friend. She called their friends. None of them drove her anywhere today. She should be at home."

"How about her office. Did she go to work today?"

"She's a teacher. Classes don't start again until tomorrow. She wouldn't leave town now."

Ashton opened the door and the four men entered the dark, quiet house. Trevor noted the officer kept his gloves on as he turned on the lights. There didn't appear to be any sign of a struggle. Trevor made a beeline for her laptop which sat on the kitchen table.

"She didn't log off." Trevor pointed to the screensaver glowing on the monitor. He tapped a few keys.

"Her manuscript is pulled up. Let me check when it was saved last." He made a couple of clicks with the mouse. "Twenty minutes after ten this morning. Of course, she may have worked a while longer."

"She mentioned to me she tries to save her work every hour to keep from losing a lot of work in case of a computer glitch." Ashton frowned at Trevor.

"So she left before noon?" Trevor asked.

"Yes." Ashton turned to the police who had searched the remaining rooms in the house.

"I'm sorry, sir. There doesn't appear to be any signs of a break in or a struggle. There isn't anything we can do right now."

Ashton threw up his hands. "But she wouldn't leave her computer on with her manuscript in plain view."

"I'm sorry, sir. Policy dictates we wait twenty-four hours unless there are signs of foul play. Please let us know if she doesn't contact you by tomorrow." The man turned and left the house.

Trevor knew his expression matched Ashton's forlorn look as the officers strode out of the house and to their car.

After pacing the floor a few times, Trevor continued. "We can't stand around here waiting for twenty-four hours."

"Agreed. Do you have a plan?"

Ashton's hopeful expression spurred Trevor to share his idea. "The reports mentioned the money from the robbery had not been recovered. The robbers didn't have it with them when they took Madison in October so they must have hidden it."

"And?" Ashton gave him a puzzled frown.

"Those two weren't the smartest guys on the block. I figure they stashed it somewhere near where their car went off the road."

Understanding came to his eyes. "Near Madison's cabin?"

"Exactly. So they'll want to go back there to retrieve it."

Ashton's expression appeared doubtful. "What makes you think they didn't already? They escaped three days ago. They may have taken her for revenge. I don't want to think what they might have already done."

"I can't think like that either. I bet they went up to the mountains and they've been there since the escape searching. They couldn't find the money."

The furrow on his brow deepened. "What? Why not?"

"Because they don't remember where they were. They were lost at the time. Now there is snow on the ground and things seem different. They need Madison to take them to the cabin so they can find where their car went off the road."

"You're kidding."

"I don't think so. Otherwise they would have done something to Madison here. If they wanted to kill her, she'd be dead on the floor. If they wanted to take her to threaten the two of us, then one of us would have gotten a call by now. The only thing left is for them to go back to the mountain where it all started."

"If you're certain, then let's go." Ashton started out the door.

Trevor put his hand on the man's shoulder. "Hold on a minute. It'll be cold up there. Snow's on the ground. Do you have any extra clothes?"

"I have some work clothes in the guest room. Sometimes I do yard work and such when I'm visiting."

"Good. Go grab them. Any boots?"

Ashton headed to the guest room. "Yes, I'll snag them and the satellite phone I let Madison use when she went to the mountains. I brought it back the other day when I visited. She plans to rent the cabin again for spring break."

Trevor strode over to the kitchen. "Great idea. I'll rummage through the pantry to see what we can use if we're going to be up there a couple of days."

In moments both men left the house with their booty. Trevor opened the back of his SUV and stowed everything.

As they left town Trevor said, "I'll need to check in with my unit to let them know I won't be in the office tomorrow."

"If they give you any trouble let me talk to them. I'll square them away if needed."

Trevor grinned at the old soldier's remark. He suspected if anyone gave him a bad time about the short notice it wouldn't take Ashton long to set them straight. "Thank you, sir, but I don't think it will be necessary."

Trevor made the call and not only did his superior allow him time off after the explanation, but he offered to grant leave to any of Trevor's fellow rangers if they decided to join him. "Thank you, sir. If anyone volunteers ask them to meet at the sheriff's office in town. I'll be sure to keep him in the loop."

"You know they have a good eight-hour head start on us. Maybe longer." Ashton tapped his fingers on the armrest as he leaned forward in the seat as if willing them to arrive sooner.

"I've been thinking about it. In the fall those men drove off the road in the dark. I don't think they'll be wandering around once the sun sets."

"They should have arrived before dark. They might have found the money by now and be long gone."

He knew the rest of Ashton's fears. That those men found the money, killed his daughter, and disappeared. "Madison is resourceful. She'd know we'd come after her."

"You're right. She's sharp as a tack. They won't outsmart her."

Trevor heard the relief in the old man's voice. He counted on the fact that she could hold her own. He had the same fears as her father, though. "Exactly. We'll arrive hours before dawn. I bet they're holed up in the same cabin where Madison stayed. Once dawn arrives they'll be out searching for the money. We'll be waiting for them."

Trevor contacted the sheriff to let him know of their suspicions.

After Trevor ended the call, he flicked a glance at Ashton. "We're on our own."

"How much firepower did you bring?"

"Everything I've got. Two 9-mm Glocks, a Weatherby rifle, a Remington R-15, and enough ammo to make sure we win."

CHAPTER TWELVE

Around four o'clock that afternoon Madison considered how stupid she'd been to answer the door without checking out the window. It probably wouldn't have changed anything. Seeing a man with a package in hand she thought UPS, especially since she expected copies of her first book. She'd been so excited she'd forgotten the warnings from her father and Trevor. Now she sat in the front passenger seat of an old Toyota, her hands and feet bound in duct tape. She shook her head, she'd done the same to these two men.

"So which way now?" Jerk One asked her.

"I'm not sure. I told you I was a passenger and didn't pay much attention on how we got there. Besides, the snow makes everything seem different. I think maybe you turn left at the next split. Or maybe it's right." Soon she'd have to give them the correct directions otherwise they'd become suspicious.

"This isn't working out like we planned." Jerk Two grumbled from the backseat.

"Shut up unless you have a better idea."

Jerk Two mumbled again, but didn't speak loud enough for Jerk One to hear.

After a few more wrong turns she could tell darkness would descend soon. She didn't want to be driving around with these idiots when that happened. "Yes, I think I remember that group of boulders. Turn right at the next Y."

Before they arrived at the cabin snow started falling again, covering the road. Then darkness fell.

Jerk One said to Jerk Two. "Cut her loose. She can walk in front of the car to make sure we don't miss the road." He stopped the vehicle.

"You heard the man. Get your ass out of the car."

Knowing her protests would not matter, Madison climbed out of the car and did as told. Her flimsy sneakers weren't meant for traipsing in snow. It didn't take long before they were soaked and her feet felt numb. She walked as quickly as possible to keep warm and arrive at their destination.

In minutes that felt like hours she finally spotted the cabin and pointed to it. She took the last of her energy to sprint the last few yards, stomping her feet on the front porch. The men followed her up the steps.

"Not so high and mighty now, are you?" Jerk Two sneered.

"Quit yacking and make a fire."

Madison said nothing. At least they wouldn't be searching for their lost money tonight. She hoped her delays would give Trevor time to locate her. Between her dad and Trevor she prayed they would figure out what happened to her and find her. Any other outcome was too scary to comtemplate.

Instead she thought about her relationship with Trevor. Her reasons for not wanting to date or marry a soldier seemed silly. Who else would she be praying for right now? An accountant or computer nerd? As nice as those men might be, they wouldn't be able to help her out of this situation.

And the kisses he'd given her. The last scorching one made her toes curl. Why had she been so stupid as to push him away?

CHAPTER THIRTEEN

The journey from Macon normally took slightly under three hours to the town nearest the cabin. Trevor and Ashton made it in two hours. From there the road became more difficult to traverse. As they traveled the elevation increased and so did the snow accumulation. Only a few inches, but it made the edge of the road even more difficult to discern in the dark.

"Someone's been up here since the last snowfall. Tire tracks." Trevor neared the first cabin.

"Someone's on foot, too." Ashton squinted through the windshield.

"I'm sure they didn't want to run off the road like last time." They crept along until the cabin where he'd spent time in October appeared. "See, the tire tracks continue. One set. They haven't come back down."

"I think you had the right idea about those dirt bags."

"Trust me, I'm almost as surprised as you." Trevor shrugged and grimaced. "I don't know about you, but I need some food and some shuteye before we start making our way to the other cabin." Trevor pulled alongside the cabin so as not to be visible from the road and stopped the vehicle.

Ashton sighed. "Being this close and not going the rest of the way doesn't feel right, but I know you are. We need to be rested and at our best before we tackle the next step."

"Let's unload everything. I don't want to start a fire in case the scent drifts toward them."

"Understood. Except for coffee, right? I hope there are plenty of blankets in the cabin."

"There are. And, yes, I think we can use the coffee pot and microwave. " They climbed out of the vehicle.

They had to break into the cabin since Trevor didn't have a key. He'd repair it later. They made quick work of their makeshift dinner. Coffee warmed them up. Ashton took the bed and Trevor the couch. He didn't expect to sleep. Running through various scenarios kept him awake. However, resting would provide the energy he'd need in the hours to come. He closed his eyes and must have drifted off. The next thing he realized, he smelled coffee brewing.

"I must be losing my touch if I didn't hear you working in the kitchen." Trevor sat up on the couch.

"Had to see if I could still do it."

Trevor put his shoes on and went into the kitchen area. "Let's hope those jerks aren't more alert than me."

"The way you and Madison described them I'm sure we'll manage fine. Glad you were able to rest. I didn't have as much luck."

Trevor furrowed his brow at Ashton's admission. "Understandable."

"So what's your plan? Hike up the road for a mile or

so then veer off into the woods?"

Trevor filled his mug with coffee. "No, we'll take the trail along the lake. It's shorter."

Taking a sip of coffee, Ashton tilted his head. "You don't think they'll expect someone coming from that direction?"

"Madison told me the robbers didn't know about it. We'll stay back and wait for them to exit then we'll follow until they find the money." Trevor rummaged through his backpack.

After a few moments Ashton said, "I agree it would be more dangerous to approach them while still in the cabin."

Trevor handed a protein bar to Ashton. "Exactly. They'll be concentrating on finding their stash."

"My priority is Madison." Ashton set his mug down on the counter and gave Trevor a stern look.

"Of course. It goes without saying. Once they find the loot they will be excited and probably less observant." Trevor frowned. "It should give Madison a better chance. I wish there was some way we could alert her we're here."

Ashton straightened his shoulders. "There is. I've been thinking about it. Years ago when she was a kid, I taught her some bird calls. I think my owl call will grab her attention.."

Trevor nodded slowly. "I remember her mentioning that. All right."

"She'll recognize it, I'm sure." Ashton bit into the protein bar with enthusiasm.

"Great. Our plan seems more and more like it will work."

"It better."

Ashton's voice sounded worried. He should be. All kinds of things could go wrong. *Stop. No negative thoughts. Madison had to make it out of this.*

They bundled up with all the clothes they had available. Trevor found ski masks for them both so they donned those as well. He took a couple of blankets and attached them to his backpack holding the extra ammo. They each carried a Glock and a rifle. The snow made their progress slow, but they managed to arrive before dawn. Putting down the blankets on the ground they crouched behind some evergreen bushes to shield them from view by anyone in the cabin.

Trevor daydreamed of the future. One with Madison. The two of them becoming more than friends. He didn't know when it had happened, but he loved her. Startled at the revelation, he almost missed the sky showing signs of the sun rise.

They caught coffee and cooking aromas drifting from the cabin.

"Good. It won't be long." Trevor whispered as he shifted his position.

Several minutes later the two men and Madison left the cabin. Madison wore a pair of jeans, sweatshirt, and tennis shoes, no coat. Trevor stifled the urge to swear, seeing her without adequate clothing.

Following the small group didn't prove challenging. The men obviously didn't think anyone else was in the area. They talked in a normal tone, arguing which direction they should search, what the rock group looked like where they hid the loot, and complained about the cold. They searched a few yards to the left of the road as they made their way toward the dead end. Each of the men carried a shovel. Good. If they had any firearms on their person they would be slowed down with their tools. He saw Madison shiver. Enough. They needed to end this. To hell with finding the money.

Trevor tapped Ashton on the shoulder indicating he should give Madison the signal. It worked. Madison's head jerked. The men kept stalking about without noticing anything amiss. Madison didn't turn in the direction of the call, but she slowed down and glanced to each side. Good. She must be searching for cover. They closed the gap between their groups.

At the same time one of the men stopped and turned back toward Madison, she dove behind some rocks. Trevor raised his rifle. "Don't move or I'll shoot."

The man facing Madison froze. The other one said, "Oh, hell, no," then took off running. Not that he could run fast in the snow. Trevor let him go. They'd find him later.

"Drop the shovel and put your hands in the air. Madison stay down." Trevor barked the orders as if he were commanding his unit.

Ashton ran toward Madison as soon as the man did as instructed. Trevor kept his rifle aimed at the man and marched toward him, being sure to keep Madison and Ashton out of the line of fire.

She threw her arms around her father. "Dad, you can't imagine how happy I am to see you."

"Oh, sweetheart, you can't be happier than I am." Ashton gave her a hug then draped the blankets around her.

"These feel heavenly." She clutched at the fabric.

Trevor kicked the shovel away from the man. "Ashton, I need you to cover him."

"Roger." He lifted his rifle and stood steady.

Making quick work with a pat down which revealed a gun in his pocket then zip tied his hands, they headed back toward the cabin where Madison had spent the night.

Trevor couldn't keep his eyes off her. Thank God they'd found her. What would those men have done once they dug up their money? He didn't want to think about it. "You must be frozen."

"I am. At least we can make a fire in the cabin where I can warm up. Do you think the other one will come back and try to shoot us?"

"I doubt it, but we'll keep watch to make sure."

Then they heard shouting followed by gun fire in the direction where the other man had run.

"Those were rifle shots along with a handgun," Ashton said, worry evident in his tone.

They crouched down behind some boulders to make sure no stray bullets found them. Moments later three sharp whistles followed by a long one erupted.

Trevor grinned. "Guess my buddies showed up after all. The series of whistles means it's all clear."

"Your buddies?" Madison asked.

"My captain told me he'd give leave to anyone who wanted to come up here and help me find you."

Madison blinked several times. "Oh. How, ah, nice. I'll have to thank them."

Trevor chuckled. "After we make it back to the cabin and warm you up."

When they arrived, two of Trevor's fellow rangers

appeared from another direction.

"Nice day for a hike in the woods," one of them said as they all entered the cabin.

"A little chilly, but not bad." Trevor chuckled.

The rangers stoked the fire and started breakfast. One of the men took the prisoner and tied him to a chair in the bedroom so they didn't have to listen to his whining.

Ashton said, "Young lady, you need to get out of those clothes and into a hot shower. I'll see what I can find for you to put on. Once you're in the bathroom toss out your clothes and I'll set them near the fire to dry."

"You can't imagine how fabulous that sounds, Dad. Thank God we figured out how to turn on the hot water tank last night." Madison raced down the hall to the bathroom.

CHAPTER FOURTEEN

"Call the sherrif. We need him to haul these guys out of here." Trevor paced the small cabin with the fire poker in one hand. Every few seconds he jabbed at the burning logs.

Ashton pulled the satellite phone out of his coat pocket. "Here, you do it. So where are the other rangers? Shouldn't they be here by now?"

Before Trevor had a chance to reply they heard the men stomping up the steps.

Trevor opened the door. "Thanks, guys. I appreciate the assist. When did you show up?"

"We followed your trail from the cabin where you left your car. We arrived here in time to see you follow someone so we circled around to approach them from the front in case something happened. And it did. Nice training exercise." They all grinned and slapped each other on the back.

"How's the lady?" the other ranger asked.

"Feels like a popsicle right now, but otherwise she's fine."

They tied the second robber to a chair and left him in the bedroom with the first one. Trevor contacted the sheriff's office.

Ashton draped Madison's clothes over a chair and set it next to the fire then rummaged through dressers and closets. Not finding any clothes he took a blanket and cut a hole in the middle and accepted a rope from one of the rangers. He passed the items to Madison when she opened the bathroom door a couple of inches. Before long she returned to the living room looking like a homeless waif, barefoot, with wet tangled hair hanging down, but a smile covering her face.

"I know I'm a fright to behold, but at least I'm warm." All the men mumbled negative responses. "And hungry. Whoever is making the food it smells wonderful. Fix me a plate, please."

They all sat at the table shoveling food in their mouths as fast as they could.

Once finished, Madison pushed back from the table. "That had to be the best meal ever."

"Thank you, ma'am. Glad you liked it."

Trevor introduced Madison to his fellow rangers.

"Now tell us what happened. We figured these guys nabbed you sometime between 10:30 and noon yesterday."

Surprise showed on her face. "You're right. How did you figure it out?"

Ashton said, "Your computer. You once mentioned you saved your manuscript at least once an hour."

"Right. Exactly. The doorbell rang about eleven o'clock. It's the usual time the UPS man arrives and I expected a package. I opened the door without thinking."

Trevor finished her description by saying, "And Jerk One and Two stood on your doorstep."

Madison grimaced. "Only one of them. Holding a package. Cap down. When I took the box he shoved me into the house and the other one came right in behind him."

Ashton patted her hand. "I know it only takes three hours to drive here. How did you keep them from searching for the money until this morning?"

Madison gave them a satisfied grin. "So you guessed they needed me to help them find the cabin."

"Anything else didn't make sense," Trevor agreed.

"I prayed you'd figure it out. So I took them up a couple of other roads. I pretended not to know the way very well. Since I didn't have a car when they found me up here, they didn't seem surprised." She chuckled. "Obviously they didn't have a better idea. We arrived after dark. God. Those last couple of miles were a nightmare. They made me walk in front of the car so they didn't drive off the road." She shivered.

Trevor's jaw ached as he clenched it hard to keep from cursing the men. "I can't tell you how sorry I am you had to go through all this."

The smile she gave them both almost blinded him. "It turned out okay, thanks to you and Dad."

Ashton held up both hands. "I'd like to take the credit, sweetheart, but I came along for the ride. Trevor figured out what they were up to and brought me here."

"Doesn't matter who had the idea. I'm glad someone did and it ended well for me. I didn't relish trying to run away from those guys in the snow with no coat and wearing sneakers."

"Hey, Lieutenant, since you have everything in hand we're going to head back down the mountain."

Trevor stood up and shook the ranger's hand along with the others. "Thanks, guys. I appreciate you fellows having my six."

"It's what we do."

Trevor turned to Ashton and Madison. "I'll head back to pick up my vehicle with these guys. You'll have time to dry out. Ashton, I'm sure you'll keep an eye on those two." Trevor motioned to the bedroom where the two robbers sat. "I should be back before the sheriff arrives."

CHAPTER FIFTEEN

While the men exited the cabin Madison enjoyed a bear crushing hug from her father.

"I don't know what I would have done if something happened to you."

She noted the unshed tears in her father's eyes.

"Trust me, I'd been trying to think of a way to escape. They aren't the smartest men I've ever met. I figured I could sneak away when they started digging for the money. My problem was my lack of warm clothes and proper shoes."

"Thanks to Trevor you didn't have to." Ashton took one of her hands in his and squeezed.

Madison took the opportunity to talk to her father. "Dad, after Mom died I—"

Ashton interrupted her. "You don't need to say anything."

"Yes, I do. I acted like a spoiled brat. Back then I was so angry that you stayed in the army and made us move again. I may still not understand everything, but I think it was your way to keep me safe and secure."

"Even before your mother died I wanted that. Afterward.... Well. I didn't know any other way."

"Thanks, Dad." Madison gave her Dad another hug.

They took the opportunity to reminisce about Madison's mother.

They heard a vehicle return about an hour later.

Trevor stomped back into the cabin shaking the snow off his shoes. "I spotted the sheriff's vehicle before I left the other cabin. They'll be here shortly."

He sat across from Madison and her father. "The men said they would flag him down and ask the sheriff to take their statements first to give you a little time."

Madison rose and checked her clothing. "These are dry enough. I'll be more comfortable wearing something other than a blanket. The shoes need a while longer." She hustled down the hallway to the bathroom.

CHAPTER SIXTEEN

"Trevor, I can't thank you enough." Ashton placed his hand on Trevor's shoulder.

He felt his face grow warm. "No need. I wouldn't be able to sleep at night if I hadn't done everything in my power to find her and bring her to safety."

Several minutes later a knock on the door sounded and Trevor opened it. "Hello, sheriff. No offense, but I hope this is the last time we meet like this." He motioned the man and his deputy into the room.

The man chuckled as he shook Trevor's hand and then Ashton's. "After your call this morning I thought the same thing."

When Madison returned to the living room they all sat down and the sheriff took Madison's statement. His deputy moved the prisoners to the police car.

Trevor listened to her account. She gave the sheriff more details than she shared earlier with him and her father. He saw her glance at the two of them during her recitation. At times he clenched his fists so tight his nails left marks on his palms. The thought of Madison being put through such an ordeal made him glad the two men were out of his reach.

After ten minutes he stood and marched into the kitchen to make a fresh pot of coffee. He didn't really want any, but he had to do something.

"Thank you again, Ms. Hendricks. I know the prosecutor will want to contact you when they go to trial."

"Will they keep the same schedule?" Madison asked the sheriff.

"Since they'll have more charges against them, I'm not certain. Someone from the District Attorney's office will be in touch."

"I suppose it doesn't matter. I'll be ready."

The sheriff rose from his chair, put on his hat, and headed toward the door. He turned. "Please Ms. Hendricks, next time you come up here don't bring those fellas with you."

They all laughed, breaking the tension.

"You can count on it, Sheriff."

Then Madison, Ashton, and Trevor cleaned up the cabin, repaired the door, and drove back to Macon.

The trip back was eerily quiet. Each of them focused on their own thoughts.

Trevor concentrated on the revelation he'd had earlier in the day. He loved Madison. They deserved to be together forever. Holding the thought close, he decided not to share it with anyone. Not even Madison. Not yet. Madison would object and he had to figure out a way to counter all her fears. And his.

CHAPTER SEVENTEEN

Madison taught school the next day. All her fellow teachers wanted the details of her ordeal. Fortunately, the students were oblivious to the reason she skipped class. She managed to work her normal schedule. She continued to struggle with thoughts of Trevor as she drove home after classes ended. He'd been so kind prior to the latest incident and he once again saved her life. How could she dismiss his attentions without appearing ungrateful?

She phoned her best friend, Joan, when she arrived home.

"I've been worried to death. Why didn't you call earlier?" Joan scolded.

"Sorry. I had so much to do in order to make it to school today I didn't call anyone after I made it home yesterday. I didn't know Dad called you." Madison used her most apologetic voice.

"As long as you tell me the whole story now I'll forgive you."

Filling Joan in on the details made the event seem even more real to Madison.

"You've been talking about Trevor for months now. How come I haven't met him?"

Madison didn't have a good response to the question. "Um, well, we usually—"

"You want to keep him to yourself, right?"

The smug tone made Madison question her own feelings even more.

"No, no. It isn't like that."

"Are you sure?"

It took a few moments before Madison replied. "Well, I thought I was."

"After what you told me I'd say he's in love with you."

Her friend's observation stunned her. "What? No. It's not true."

"Why not? Why else would he drive up a snowy mountain in the middle of the night? After calling your father and then the police, most men would say they'd done enough. Not your ranger. He had the skills to rescue you and it doesn't sound like he hesitated a moment."

The same thoughts had been swirling around in Madison's head. "You may be right."

Joan's voice became soft and serious. "And you?"

After a deep sigh Madison admitted, "I've been trying to figure it out."

"I know what you think about relationships with military men. Doesn't that seem ridiculous now?"

Joan's question hit Madison between the eyes. "Maybe."

"Even if you marry some accountant you may have to move. A lot of people are transferred to other locations for their jobs. Your insistance on having a forever home sounds unrealistic. It doesn't happen often anymore."

What did she want from Trevor? The moment she realized the dangerous situation she found herself in he became her beacon of hope. She prayed for rescue. Her father had been the second person she thought of. A distant second. The fact they were both military men didn't escape her notice. Not only would they be the first to recognize her missing status, she knew they would move heaven and earth to find her. And they did. She knew her chances of survival without their help had been slim.

Were her emotions due to gratitude? Or had she fallen in love with a soldier?

CHAPTER EIGHTEEN

"Yes, sir. Thank you, sir." Trevor saluted his captain and left the room.

In the hallway one of the men who assisted with Madison's rescue ambled toward him. "Lieutenant, sir. How's your lady doing?"

Trevor grinned at the idea of Madison as his lady. "She's fine. Again, thanks for your help."

"You had it covered, sir. We just finished picking up the trash." The ranger laughed at his own lame joke.

Trevor chuckled. As he continued down the hall toward his office his thoughts turned serious. He'd been struggling with the notion of calling Madison. It would be better to not see or talk to her again. He'd already decided no good would come out of it. He knew how she felt about military men. And he didn't think a ranger should be married. This was the end.

A fellow officer who shared his office interrupted Trevor's musings a few minutes later. "How come the long face?"

"What? Oh, nothing." Trevor shuffled the papers on

his desk to cover his momentary unease. He tried to concentrate on the unit's budget. His duty when not on deployment.

"I figured after your heroic efforts there would be celebrations and some hot monkey sex with the damsel you rescued."

He frowned at the crude remark about Madison. "It's not like that between us." He knew his voice conveyed more than annoyance.

The other man threw up his arms as if in surrender. "Hey, don't bite my head off. Sorry. Guess she must be *the one*."

"*The one* what?" Realization dawned. "No. Can't be. She doesn't date military guys and I don't believe in marriage for rangers." Uh-oh. The other man had a wife.

He didn't take offense, but offered his opinion. "Most of the time I'd agree. We have a tough job. Being married to one of us isn't easy. However, it sounds like you have a special lady. One who might have escaped on her own without help. Someone who knows what it means to be left behind. How to deal."

Trevor couldn't keep his curiosity to himself. "So how did you and your wife figure it out?"

"She's an army brat, too. Knew what to expect. And I knew I couldn't live without her."

"No problems?" He couldn't keep the skepticism out of his voice.

With a bark of laughter the other man shrugged. "Of course we have problems. What married couple doesn't? We work through them. Sometimes we have to be more creative in how we resolve things. If you love each other it's what you do." The officer turned back to his computer and began typing.

Would Madison think their relationship worth the work? And risk? For that matter, did he?

CHAPTER NINETEEN

"How's my girl?"

"Great, Dad. What's up?" Madison tried to sound upbeat. Her father made a point of calling around six o'clock every evening since they'd returned from the mountains.

"Wondering when you're coming for a visit."

She hesitated before answering. "Not this weekend. How about the weekend after?"

"Perfect. So what's bothering you?"

She laughed at her father's astute ear. "What makes you ask?"

"I can hear it in your voice."

She had no desire to pour out her inner thoughts. "Nothing. Simply trying to work out the next scene in my book."

"And I'm Santa Claus."

"I said it was nothing." She stood up and paced the living room.

"All right. I'll give it a rest. You know you can talk through anything with me. Whatever or, perhaps I should say, whoever it is."

"Never mind. See you next week." Madison ended their call.

Perhaps she should talk to her father about Trevor. He and her mom seemed happy in their marriage in spite of the deployments and constant moving. She wished her mother were still alive. It would be easier to talk with her. Hear the woman's side of the situation.

The days flew by and she found herself thinking about Trevor again on her drive to Columbus to visit her dad. Trevor hadn't called since he'd dropped her off after their latest trip to the mountains. She smiled when thinking about the mountains. They always calmed her worries. Their love of the Blue Ridge Mountains was something she and Trevor shared. In spite of the harrowing events the last two times she'd been there, they still meant peace and tranquility to her.

Once she arrived at her father's house he flung open the door before Madison managed to take her suitcase out of the trunk. "What were you doing? Watching out the window?" She laughed and allowed him to pick up her luggage.

"I happened to walk by it when you pulled up."

They strolled together into the house. As they entered, Madison sniffed the air. "Yum. What are you cooking? It smells delicious."

"Your mother's lasagna."

"I should have guessed. Considering how much the recipe makes I know I'll be able to take some home. Great! Leftovers for me next week."

"Exactly. For both of us."

They chatted for a while. Her father poured them each a glass of wine. Moments later the doorbell rang.

"I hope you don't mind. I invited someone else to have dinner with us." Her father strolled to the front door.

Before she had time to figure out who the other guest might be, he flung open the door and there stood Trevor holding a bottle of wine.

"More wine. Perfect. Come in and I'll pour you a glass of what we're having. Madison and I were chatting. Join us."

"Yes, sir. I didn't realize your daughter would be here." He turned to her. "Hi. How's your writing?"

"Fine. Good to see you."

An uncomfortable silence followed. Ashton busied himself in the kitchen with no apparent desire to bridge the gap. Trevor took a seat across from her. She noticed his face had a red tint to it. Was he embarrased? Or was there some other reason for the flush?

"Mr. Hendricks, sir, if you and your daughter want to dine alone I understand. We can do this another time."

"No, no. I insist you stay. This is a thank-you dinner for Trevor, Madison. I knew you would want to be included."

"Of course. Yes. Great idea, Dad. I should have thought of it."

He shook a finger at her. "Yes, you should have."

Madison swallowed the lump in her throat at the admonishment.

They ate in relative silence. Her father ignored their apparent unease and lack of appetite. He finally stood up and took his plate to the sink. Returning to the table, he started clearing everything. “I think you two have spent enough time pushing your food around. Dinner is over. I don’t mean to be pushy. Well, yes, I suppose I am. The two of you should talk. I’ll take care of the dishes. Trevor, take Madison for a drive and talk things over.”

Madison’s cheeks grew warm and she knew her face must be as red as Trevor’s.

“Yes, sir.” He held out his hand to Madison.

They nodded to her father and left.

“Sorry. I don’t know why he did that.” Madison speared Trevor with an apologetic glance as soon as the door closed behind them.

“I’m not sorry. I’ve been wanting to talk to you and didn’t know if I should call.” They climbed into his SUV and Trevor started driving.

“Talk about what?”

He gazed at her meaningfully. “I think you know.”

She fidgeted and looked down at her hands. “I suppose I do. I think I might owe you an apology.”

“Apology? I can’t think why.” He frowned and appeared puzzled.

She forced herself to look him in the eyes. “When we first met I said I wouldn’t date anyone in the military.”

“Yes, I know. It’s why I’ve been hesitating to call.”

Madison shifted in her seat as much as the seatbelt allowed. “The more I thought about it, the more I realized how foolish my notion was.”

“You did?”

Did she hear relief in his voice?

“Yes, and I think I hurt you for a silly reason.”

“I have a confession to make, too.”

"Oh, what?"

"I did want to date you."

Her stomach felt like it dropped through the floor. "Did? Is that past tense?"

"I'm not sure. We need to talk. Really talk about why you don't want to date a military man. And I need to explain some of my concerns."

Arriving at a coffee shop, they paused their conversation until they entered and ordered lattes.

Trevor returned to their discussion. "So what is your silly reason for not dating men in the military?"

Sighing, she looked at her hands. "While growing up I hated the way we moved every two or three years. It's like we didn't have a permanent home. I don't have any friends from childhood. I'm lonesome at times."

"You said you changed your mind."

"Yes, I did. A lot of jobs cause a person to move. Not only the army. I finally recognized your family is your home. Mother always made any place we stayed a home. Other army wives and their kids were always around. When she died my junior year in high school things changed. I became lonesome. Now that I recognize the difference, I'm sure I could make it work." She gazed into Trevor's eyes.

He smiled for the first time. "Sounds like you want to."

"Exactly. Like my mother must have."

"You can't imagine how much it means to me that you shared your feelings. I need to explain my concerns. I never thought a permanent relationship was a good idea for a ranger. For some of the reasons you mentioned. The biggest objection is the possibility the soldier won't come home. That's why I hesitate about commitments."

"So you've changed your mind, too?" Did she dare hope?

"I talked to one of the married guys. He said it's something two people have to talk about and agree to the risks. Like all the other risks in a relationship."

"Like what we're doing right now?"

"Exactly. So, do you want to give it a try knowing all this?"

She knew her smile must be a mile wide. "Yes. I can't imagine not seeing you again."

"Let's get out of here." Trevor paid the bill and they almost flew back to his SUV. Once inside Trevor gathered Madison in his arms and kissed her the way she'd been dreaming about for months.

Several minutes later he broke the kiss. "Whew. I have to take you back to your dad's. We better wait for another time to continue this."

Grinning like a couple of fools, they drove back to Madison's father's house. Slowly. Very slowly and in a round about way.

Trevor strolled with Madison to the door. "Tomorrow afternoon?"

"Yes, I'll be ready."

Madison watched as Trevor walked back to his truck and drove away. She stood at the door watching until she could no longer see his tail lights. Most definitely, she'd be ready.

CHAPTER TWENTY

Trevor spent Sunday morning on the phone making arrangements. With only thirty minutes left before his first official date with Madison he showered, shaved, and then put on fresh clothes. He relaxed and smiled. This would work. It had to.

Arriving precisely at noon, he rang the doorbell.

Ashton answered the door. “Trevor, come in. So glad you and Madison have seen the light.”

“Thank you for pushing us, sir.”

He heard Madison’s voice as she walked down the hall. “I’m ready. Where are we going? Bye, Dad.”

“Wow. You look fantastic.”

“Thank you. I’m glad I packed this.”

They walked to his SUV where Trevor opened her door.

“I made reservations at a Greek resturant. You once said you liked lamb.”

“Yum. Yes, indeed. I love it.”

They talked about general topics on the way to the restaurant. During their meal, Trevor’s phone rang. The call he'd been expecting.

"Thank you. Yes, I can sign the papers tomorrow." He disconnected the call.

"Your smile must mean that was good news."

"Great news, actually."

"About the robbers?"

"No. Good lord, I hope I never hear about those guys again. Except for the trial. Although I suppose I should thank them."

Her stunned expression almost made him laugh.

"Thank them? Whatever for?"

"For bringing you to me. You remember the cabin where we caught up with those guys?"

"How could I forget?" She frowned and tilted her head. "What about it?"

"I made a deal with the owner. He sold me the place."

Shock appeared on her face. "You bought a cabin in the Blue Ridge Mountains?"

"As soon as I sign the papers."

"Oh, that's great." Her expression didn't match her words. "I suppose you'll be spending all your spare time up there now."

"I sure hope so." Did she think he didn't want her with him?

He rushed to explain. "I know it isn't a place where we'd live full time, but no matter where the army sends me we'd have it to return to. Maybe have Christmas there every year. Unless I'm deployed. So what do you say?"

"Us?"

"Exactly. The two of us. I bought it so we'll have a

forever home. Like what you've always wanted. You'll have to marry me, though." He held his breath for her answer.

"Oh, Trevor. You listened to me. Really listened. To what I really wanted. Of course I'll marry you."

He exhaled in relief. "Perfect."

Trevor closed the distance between them to seal their promise with a kiss.

ABOUT THE AUTHOR

Rebecca Bridges spent eight years in the U.S. Army Reserves as a Warrant Officer. Her husband is a retired army officer. Having experience from both sides of the army family she can't imagine living any other kind of life.

Rebecca and her husband retired to the coast of South Carolina where the ocean waves and palmetto trees feed their souls. Writing, golfing, traveling and playing with their grandchildren keep them busy and fulfilled.

Rebecca loves to hear from anyone who's read her work. Please contact her at her website:

www.RebeccaBridgesAuthor.com

98662786R00074

Made in the USA
Columbia, SC
03 July 2018